ABOUT THE ALDEN ALL STARS

Nothing's more important to Derrick, Matt, Josh, and Jesse than their team, the Alden Panthers. Whether the sport is football, hockey, baseball, or track–and–field, the four seventh-graders can always be found practicing, sweating, and giving their all. Sometimes the Panthers are on their way to a winning season, and sometimes the team can't do anything right. But no matter what, you can be sure the Alden All Stars are playing to win.

"This fast-paced [series] is sure to be a hit with young readers."   —*Publishers Weekly*

"Packed with play-by-play action and snappy dialogue, the text adeptly captures the seventh-grade sports scene."   —*ALA Booklist*

The *Alden All Stars* series:

Hotshot on Ice

David Halecroft

PUFFIN BOOKS

PUFFIN BOOKS
Published by the Penguin Group
Viking Penguin, a division of Penguin Books USA Inc.,
375 Hudson Street, New York, New York 10014, U.S.A.
Penguin Books Ltd, 27 Wrights Lane, London W8 5TZ, England
Penguin Books Australia Ltd, Ringwood, Victoria, Australia
Penguin Books Canada Ltd, 10 Alcorn Avenue, Ontario, Canada M4V 3B2
Penguin Books (N.Z.) Ltd, 182–190 Wairau Road, Auckland 10, New Zealand

Penguin Books Ltd, Registered Offices: Harmondsworth, Middlesex, England

First published in Puffin Books, 1991
1 3 5 7 9 10 8 6 4 2
Copyright © Daniel Weiss and Associates, 1991
All rights reserved

Library of Congress Catalog Card Number: 91-53026
ISBN 0-14-034907-3

Printed in the United States of America
Set in Century Schoolbook

1

Derrick Larson was ready. His knees were bent, his eyes were on the puck.

"Show us your stuff, Derrick," Coach Campbell shouted, whacking a fast pass to center ice.

Derrick hooked the puck with his stick and charged toward the goal. He drove his hips from side to side, digging his skate blades into the ice to pick up speed. It was a one-on-one drill, Derrick versus the defenseman.

Derrick stickhandled, tapping the puck back and

forth, while keeping his eyes on the defenseman. The defenseman was a new kid of average height and medium build, with brown hair sticking out from beneath a big white helmet. Derrick had watched the new kid warm up. In Derrick's opinion, the kid didn't look like much of a hockey player.

By the time he crossed the blue line, Derrick was racing with long smooth strides. He cut sharply toward the new player, picking up speed as he turned. Derrick figured he'd just fake a slap shot, take the new kid out of the play, then flip the puck over the goalie's shoulder and into the net.

When the new player got close enough, Derrick lifted his stick to fake the shot. But instead of lunging toward the fake, the new kid kept skating right toward Derrick, crouching low to deliver a hip check. Derrick could hardly believe it, and his blue eyes opened wide in surprise. He tried to cut toward the boards to get out of the way, but he wasn't fast enough—and he felt a solid hip ram into his side.

Derrick lost his balance and went up on one skate, tipping backward and swinging his arms wildly. Finally his skate slipped out from under him, and Derrick slammed to the ice. He slid all the way into the crease, knocked the goalie over, and ended up in a heap in the back of the net.

The rest of the Panthers were trying hard to keep from laughing at Derrick, who looked like a huge fish caught in a fisherman's net.

"I can't believe it!" Derrick muttered, as he untangled himself from the net. He watched the new kid skate up ice, stickhandling the puck like a pro. "Who *is* that guy?"

It was the first practice of Alden Junior High's eighth-grade hockey team. The Cranbrook Municipal Rink was all lit up, and the ice was shiny, white, and new. A long row of windows stretched above the empty stands, and the winter sky outside was already turning dark. Derrick had been waiting for this day all autumn. It had felt great to lace up his skates, tape up his hockey stick, and hit the ice for another season as the Alden Panthers' star center.

This season, Derrick had something to prove. It had to do with a guy named Davey Schonberg. Schonberg was the star center on the rival Williamsport hockey team, a big, lanky boy with a wicked slap shot. Last season, Schonberg had walked away with the conference high-scoring trophy—leaving Derrick in the dust.

This season, Derrick wanted to prove that he was the best player in the conference. He wanted to take home that shiny high-scoring trophy and put it with

3

the rest of his trophies on his bedroom windowsill.

Derrick had a big solid frame with powerful legs and arms—a perfect hockey player's body. He was friendly, with light blond hair and a good sense of humor, but when it came to hockey, Derrick didn't like being second best.

Derrick had grown up in Minnesota, the heart of hockey country, and he had played on the Minnesota State Championship hockey team. Last season, however, Derrick had left Minnesota and moved to Cranbrook, and that's when the problems started. The Alden Panthers weren't nearly as good as Derrick's old team, and Derrick had felt his skills slipping with every practice. He had ended up having the worst season of his life, and Schonberg had easily snatched the scoring title.

Still, Derrick had helped teach the team how to skate and shoot, and had really helped the Panthers improve. Derrick even thought that this year, the Panthers stood an outside chance of making it to the championship. That would be the ultimate thrill. But Derrick told himself not to let his hopes get too high.

Derrick was much more hopeful about winning the scoring title. He *knew* that he was good enough. If he could bring that trophy home, then he would prove to himself—and to everybody else—that he hadn't lost all his skills last season, and that he really *was* the best player in the conference.

The only problem was the Alden Panthers. Even though the guys on the team had improved, they still weren't the greatest hockey players. To beat Schonberg for the high-scoring trophy, he'd need to have a great left winger and a great right winger— guys who could feed him passes, and help make the big plays.

Derrick skated back to the line, rubbing a big new bruise on his thigh. He watched the new kid turn with the puck, then skate back toward the team wearing a little smile. Derrick wondered if this new kid might be just what the Panthers needed.

Coach blew his whistle and skated onto the ice.

"Nice hip check, Chris," Coach said to the new player, who was speeding toward the team. "I think you gave Derrick a real surprise. Everybody, take a minute to meet Chris Santini, the newest Alden Panther. Chris just moved to Cranbrook from Michigan, so let's give him a big hello."

Chris turned to the side and screeched to a perfect stop right next to Derrick and his two best friends, Josh Bank and Woody Franklin.

"No hard feelings?" Chris asked Derrick, smiling

to reveal teeth covered with silver braces. "I didn't mean to knock you into the net."

"I guess I was pretty surprised," Derrick answered, rubbing his bruise. "I'm just not used to getting knocked off my skates like that."

"I was pretty surprised, too," Josh Bank said. "I was watching you warm up, and I thought you skated more like a figure skater than a hockey player."

Chris laughed. "Well, I *used* to be a figure skater, when I was younger. I still warm up with some of my old figure-skating exercises."

"If you ask me," Josh said, "figure skating is for girls."

Chris's face turned red. "For your information, a lot of boys figure skate," Chris answered, sounding a little angry.

"Maybe so," Josh said, shrugging his shoulders. "But only if they're not tough enough to play good, hard hockey."

Derrick elbowed Josh in the ribs. Josh was scrawny, but he had the biggest mouth in Alden Junior High. Josh was liable to say anything that popped into his mind. Derrick didn't want Josh to get the new kid any angrier.

"Hey Chris," Derrick said, quickly changing the subject, "what position do you play?"

"I'll play wherever Coach Campbell puts me," Chris answered. "I just want to play hockey." Chris turned to Josh and stared him right in the eye. "Good, hard hockey."

Derrick laughed and smiled at Chris. Derrick liked anybody who stood up to Josh's big mouth. He gave Chris a little thumbs-up.

"And what position do *you* play?" Chris asked Josh. "You look like a defenseman to me."

"A defenseman?" Josh snapped, his face turning red. "I'm no defenseman. I'm a left winger. I score goals."

The year before, Derrick, Woody, and Josh had been the Panthers' first team front line. Derrick had been center, with Woody at right wing and Josh at left wing. The three friends had started calling themselves the Three Musketeers.

"And this season," Josh went on, smacking his stick against the ice, "the Three Musketeers will rule the ice!"

"All for one, and one for all!" came a shout from behind them. They spun around to see a big fat player skating right toward Josh's back. It was Bannister, the class clown, with his arm raised, carrying his stick like a sword. He wasn't a very good athlete, but everyone on the team liked him for his sense of humor. Bannister tried to stop an inch away from Josh, but instead he smacked Josh in the back and sent him sprawling forward. Josh landed on his face on the ice.

"Make that the *Two* Musketeers," Bannister said, laughing as he helped Josh up.

Derrick looked over to Chris and tried to keep from cracking up.

"Bannister, one of these days, I'm going to . . ." Josh said, shaking his fist under Bannister's double chin.

"Okay, men, enough fooling around," Coach Campbell said, blowing his whistle. "We've got a big season in front of us. And in that last drill, Chris showed us what the season will be all about. *Checking*. Tough, hard checking."

According to conference rules, eighth grade was the first year that players could use hip checks and body checks. Derrick couldn't wait for the season to begin, so he could finally start knocking players to the ice, slamming them against the boards, and stealing the puck away—just like Wayne Gretsky.

"This year is going to be a lot rougher than last year," Coach went on. "We're going to have to be mean on the ice."

That sounded good to Derrick. He looked over to Chris. Chris nodded in return.

"Let's get back to the drill, men," Coach Campbell said, tapping his pencil on his clipboard. "Chris, go back on defense. Josh, your turn to try a shot on goal."

"Good," Josh said to Derrick, pulling his hockey gloves on tighter. "I want to show Chris what a real left winger can do."

Chris skated back into position near the net. Derrick watched Josh get Coach's pass, and rush toward the goal with the puck. Josh wasn't as quick on his skates as Derrick, but he was a good faker. As Chris skated forward, Josh faked a shot, then tried to sprint around Chris toward the goal. Chris changed direction with him, crouched down, and smacked Josh right in the chest. Josh lost his balance, slammed to the ice, and slid all the way into the boards, where he crashed into a pile. Chris recovered the loose puck, turned a perfect turn, and stickhandled the puck across the blue line.

Josh was fuming when he got back in line, next to Derrick and Woody.

"Did you see that?" Josh said. "That was an illegal check. If this had been a game, the ref would have called charging."

9

"I was watching," Woody said. "And Chris didn't charge. He only took *two* steps toward you, before he creamed you. If he had taken *three* steps, then it would have been charging."

"I know the rules," Josh said, "and I say it was charging."

"Admit it, Josh," Derrick said, nudging his friend playfully in the side. "Chris beat you fair and square."

"Josh!" Coach called out, marking something down on his clipboard. "I want you to go in at defense, and give Chris a crack at the goal."

"Defense?" Josh muttered under his breath, as he skated off toward the goal. "I hate defense. I'm a winger."

A moment later, Chris started off with the puck from the center line. When Chris came close enough to the goal to try a wrist shot, Josh put his shoulder down and tried to drive it into Chris's chest. Chris cut to the side—and Josh went flying forward into the air.

Now it was one on one—Chris against the goalie, A.J. Pape. Chris sped toward the net, and A.J. put his knee pads together, ready to burst in either direction for the save. Chris made a fake toward the high left corner of the net. When A.J. leaped to the left, Chris flicked the puck high to the other side, right into the corner of the goal.

Chris made it look so easy.

"Nice goal, Chris," Coach said. "And Josh, I want you to stay at defense for a while."

Derrick smiled as he watched Chris skate toward the team, racing in long confident strides. He was psyched to have Chris on the team. He knew that Chris could help the Panthers get to the championship—and help him beat Schonberg for the scoring title.

"Oh, Coach?" Chris said, stopping in the middle of the ice. "I have something to tell the team. Something important."

"Go ahead," Coach said, looking concerned.

The ice grew quiet, and all eyes fell on Chris.

" 'Chris' is just a nickname," Chris said, looking down at the ice. "My real name is Christina."

"Christina?" the whole team asked, confused.

"Yes," Chris said, taking off her helmet. "I'm a girl."

2

After practice that afternoon, Derrick, Josh, Woody, and Bannister hurried to the Game Place to talk about the big news. The Game Place was in the Cranbrook Mall, not far from the Municipal Rink. The crowded gameroom was filled with the sounds of racing engines, machine guns, and exploding bombs. Pinball machines added beeps and bells to the racket, and some of the games even talked out loud in weird computer voices.

"We just *can't* have a girl on our hockey team,"

Josh said. He spun a knob, and a little metal hockey player slapped a shot on goal. Derrick jerked his goalie over and blocked the puck.

"It's just not right!" Josh continued. "You don't see any girls playing on the Boston Bruins, do you? Or the Minnesota North Stars?"

The four friends were standing in the back of the gameroom by the pinball machines, playing their favorite knob hockey game. They were supposed to be playing a game of two-on-two, Derrick and Bannister versus Josh and Woody, but the argument had gotten so hot that no one was really paying attention.

"You guys are so old-fashioned," Bannister said, looking amazed. "Chris may be a girl, but she's a good hockey player. We have to give her a chance."

Derrick passed the puck from his goalie to his right winger, and thought about Chris. He knew that Chris was a good player, who could skate well and check like a demon.

On the other hand, it seemed kind of weird having a girl on the hockey team. In fact, it seemed downright *wrong*. Derrick knit his brow and moved the puck into shooting position.

"I'll bet girls aren't even *allowed* to play in our league," Woody said, moving his defenseman over to block Derrick. "I'll bet there's some rule about that."

"No way," Bannister said. "Remember what Coach Campbell said this afternoon? He said there was a girl on Cranbrook High's varsity football team, so there was no reason why there couldn't be a girl on our hockey team. Besides, Coach knows all the rules—and he was psyched to have Chris on the team."

"We'll be the laughing stock of the conference," Josh said. "If we have a girl on the team, people are going to wonder why the Panthers don't wear cute pink uniforms."

"And why we don't put little bows and ribbons in our hair," Woody added.

"What do you think, Derrick?" Josh asked.

Derrick looked down at the board and took a deep breath.

"All I care about is that the Panthers win the conference championship," Derrick said. "And that I win the conference high-scoring trophy."

"But what about Chris?" Bannister asked.

Derrick shrugged.

"She's a girl," Derrick answered, adjusting his player. "I just don't think we can play *real* hockey with a girl on the team."

Derrick quickly snapped his wrist. His player spun around, whacked the puck, and sent it flying toward the goal. Josh jerked his goalie over, but a red marker went up on top of the net, to show that a goal had been scored.

"So what are we going to do?" Woody asked, popping the puck out of the net. "How are we going to convince Coach that we can't play hockey with a girl?"

"It's simple," Josh said, leaning in and lowering his voice. "All we have to do is *treat* her like a girl. We won't check her, because we're afraid to hurt her. We won't joke around with her, because we're scared we might hurt her feelings. Once Coach sees how differently we treat her, he'll put her on the bench for sure. Maybe even cut her from the team. How's that?"

"Sounds good to me," Woody answered.

"Me too, I guess," Derrick said, shrugging.

"I think you guys are making a big mistake," Bannister argued, holding the plastic puck above the board for a faceoff. "But I'll keep my big fat mouth shut."

"Besides," Josh said, looking at Derrick and Woody. "We have to keep the Three Musketeers together, right?"

Bannister dropped the puck, and Derrick and Josh slashed back and forth, fighting for control. Finally,

Derrick smacked the puck back to Bannister's defenseman. Bannister passed back to Derrick's center iceman, and Derrick flicked the puck into the corner of the goal.

The little red marker went up again.

"With Derrick on the Panthers," Woody said with a smile, "We *can't* lose."

"As long as we don't have any girls on our team, too," Josh added.

"Skating is the most important skill in hockey," Coach Campbell said, the next day at practice. "A team that can skate well, wins. It's that simple. Now, let's see what you can do. We'll start with wind sprints, six times back and forth."

The whole team lined up at the side boards, and took off at the sound of Coach's whistle. Derrick charged forward, digging his skates into the ice, and keeping an eye on Chris—who was skating right beside him. Derrick wanted to make sure that he stayed well in front of Chris, and he hoped that Josh and Woody could do the same.

Derrick made it to the opposite boards two strides ahead of everyone else. He came to a complete stop, touched the boards with his glove, then spun around and began to charge back. When he looked over his shoulder, Chris was right behind him. Josh and Woody had fallen four strides back and were struggling to keep up.

When the drill was over, Derrick stopped and leaned against the boards to catch his breath. Chris finished next, with Woody and Josh and the rest of the Panthers following behind. Chris looked over to Derrick with a smile.

"You sure can skate," Chris said. "You're definitely the one to beat on this team. Where'd you learn to skate like that?"

Just as Derrick was about to answer, Josh grabbed Derrick's arm and pulled him away. Chris was left standing by herself, looking over at the boys with a confused expression.

"You remember what we agreed," Josh whispered as he pulled Derrick toward the boys. "We have to show Coach that Chris just doesn't fit in on the team."

"Admit it, Josh," Bannister said, his chest heaving from the wind sprints. "You're just mad because she can skate faster than you."

Before Josh could answer, Coach Campbell blew his whistle and called the team to attention.

"Listen up," Coach began. "We have our first game next week, against Williamsport. That doesn't give us much time to get ready. Williamsport has some fine players—Davey Schonberg, for instance."

Derrick cringed at the name Davey Schonberg.

"We'll have to be good checkers," Coach continued. "Now, checking is the essence of defense. It's the part of hockey that the fans like best, too. But it's not easy. Let's see how much you know about checking, before we start the next drill." Coach looked down at his clipboard. "First of all, what *is* a check?"

Derrick spoke right up. "A check is when you knock somebody to the ice to steal the puck away. But there are other kinds of checks, too. Like the poke check, where you try to steal the puck away by poking at it with your stick."

"Good," Coach said. "But that was an easy question. Now, when should you *never* try to check a player?"

Coach looked around the team, but no one was answering. Finally Chris raised her hand and spoke up.

"You should never check when you're the last player protecting the goalie," Chris answered tentatively. "Because if you miss the check, then the player with the puck will have an easy shot on the goal."

Coach looked impressed. "That's right, Chris.

Never check unless there's somebody else behind you to pick up the puck-handler, in case you miss." Coach nodded and glanced back down at his clipboard. "Okay, when you're going to check somebody, what should you keep your eyes on?"

Josh spoke up. "The puck, because that's what you're trying to steal."

"No way," Chris answered, raising her hand. "You should keep your eyes right on the player's chest, because a player can't fake you out with his chest. But he can fake you out with his stick or his eyes or his legs."

"Right again, Chris," Coach said, lifting his eyebrows.

Derrick had to admit that Chris knew her stuff. He glanced over to Josh and saw that his friend's face had turned red.

"Let's try a checking drill," Coach said, skating out to center ice with a puck. "Josh, you and Sam Kruger start off as defensemen. Chris and Derrick, you'll be the offense. A.J., in at goal."

"Defense again," Josh muttered angrily, slapping his stick against the ice. He turned to Derrick and whispered. "Remember what I said about taking it easy on Chris? Well, forget it. I don't care if she's a girl or not, I'm going to check her as hard as I can."

Derrick laughed, straightened his knee pads, and got ready for action. The drill was simple—Derrick and Chris would charge toward the goal, passing back and forth, while Josh and Sam tried to slam them with body checks.

When everyone was ready, Coach blew his whistle and Derrick started off. Immediately, Sam rushed over to check Derrick, crouching down and leading with his shoulder. Derrick twisted his body to the side, and Sam spun off into the boards. Then Derrick flicked a pass back to Chris, who was speeding across the ice in his direction.

Chris took the pass and cut toward the goal. Josh was ready for her. He skated backward, poke checking the puck with his stick. When she faked left and charged right, Josh turned to the right as well, then drove his whole shoulder and side into Chris. Chris lost her balance and smashed to the ice, while the puck went skidding off toward the far boards. Josh tripped on Chris's leg and flipped forward onto the ice, sprawling out spread-eagle and tossing his stick to the side before he could reach the puck.

Chris was back up on her skates in a split-second, while Josh hurried off to pick up his stick. Chris got control of the puck and charged the goal. She pumped a fake slap shot, then flicked a perfect wrist shot into the corner of the goal, right above A.J.'s shoulder.

Coach blew his whistle. "Remember, Josh. Don't check someone when you're the last player in front of the goal. You just learned why. If something goes wrong, the offensive player will have an easy shot on goal. And Chris, nice recovery."

Derrick couldn't help but be impressed with Chris's play. Still, he and his friends had made an agreement. Chris had to go, and that was that.

No matter how well she plays, Derrick thought, *she's still a girl.*

3

"Uh-oh," Derrick muttered, "Josh isn't going to like this."

Derrick and Woody were staring at the final lineup for today's game, which was thumbtacked to the door of the boys' locker room. The two friends stood with their hockey sticks across their shoulders and their skates in their hands, shaking their heads.

"It's the end of the Three Musketeers," Woody said.

The first team front line was Derrick at center,

Woody at right wing—and Chris Santini at left wing. Josh had lost his position to Chris, and was going to play defenseman with Sam Kruger. The second team front line was Jack Prall, Dave McShea, and Alex Kroll. The second team defensemen were Bannister and Mike Willis, and the goalie was A.J. Pape.

Derrick was bummed, but deep down, he wasn't all that surprised. He knew that Chris was a better skater than Josh, and probably a better checker. Still, how could the Panthers do well—and how could *he* beat Schonberg—with a girl on the ice?

Derrick heard a loud, high banshee cry and turned around to see Josh rushing toward the door. Josh was stickhandling a tennis ball in front of him, dodging and cutting as he ran, his bright red hair streaming out behind. Finally he whacked the ball against the door, right between Derrick and Woody.

"Goal!" Josh said with a smile, catching the ball on the rebound. As soon as Josh saw the expressions on his two friends' faces, his smile disappeared. "What's wrong?" he asked, leaning in to read the roster.

Derrick watched as Josh's face went pale. Josh dropped his gym bag and hockey stick to the floor.

"I don't believe it," he said angrily. "I lost my position to a *girl?*"

Josh spun around and chucked the ball as far as he could down the hallway, shouting in frustration. At that moment, Chris came around the corner. She saw the ball coming, snapped out her hand, and snagged an amazing catch.

"You're out!" Chris laughed, jerking her thumb into the air, then tossing the ball back to Josh. "Hey, is that the lineup for today's game?"

No one answered. Josh shoved the ball into his pocket, gave Chris a cold glance, and disappeared into the locker room.

"What's wrong with him?" Chris asked.

Derrick and Woody didn't answer either. They followed Josh into the boys' locker room, leaving Chris alone in the hallway.

The locker room was loud with talk and banging lockers. Chris changed in the girls' locker room, down the hall, and Derrick was relieved to have a few minutes with only the guys around. Still, he caught himself feeling a little sorry for Chris. He knew it couldn't be much fun to get the cold shoulder from a whole team.

"At least she can't come into our locker room,"

Woody said, as he pulled his uniform from his athletic bag.

"Williamsport is going to laugh us out of the rink when they learn we've got a girl on the front line," Derrick added, sitting down to untie his shoes.

"Those guys will never know Chris is a girl," Bannister said, walking up. "Williamsport is going to treat her like any other player, so why shouldn't we?"

"Because she's a girl, that's why," Josh said. "Anyway, I've got a plan." Josh lowered his voice. "We've got to make Chris look bad in the game today. That way, Coach will put me back on the front line. So let's just never pass to Chris, even if she's open. Let's just keep the puck to ourselves, and rack up the points for the Three Musketeers."

Woody and Derrick nodded their agreement, even though Derrick didn't think it would work.

Derrick pulled on his thick, padded pants and strapped the suspenders over his shoulders. He pulled on his blue and gold Alden jersey, then adjusted his shoulder pads, elbow pads, and shin guards. As he tied up his skates, Derrick thought about Josh's plan. He hoped it worked—but he knew from experience that most hockey games didn't turn out as planned.

Derrick slammed Davey Schonberg into the boards, pinning him against the Plexiglas. He drove his shoulder into Schonberg's back and kicked at the loose puck with his skate.

"Nice try, Larson," Schonberg grunted under his breath. "But this game is *mine*."

Derrick kicked the puck free, then stickhandled across the blue line and into the Panthers' offensive zone. He glanced around the ice, checking out the defense. Both defensemen skated out to meet Derrick, but Chris was speeding down the left side, open for a pass. She cut toward the goal, all alone. Even though she was totally open, Derrick didn't pass.

Instead he lifted his stick for a wild slap shot— and *wham!* Schonberg body-checked him from behind, just as another defenseman hip-checked him in front. Derrick flew through the air like a human cannonball, while his stick twirled off and crashed against the boards. When he got back onto his skates, Schonberg was stickhandling the puck across the center line, speeding into the Panthers' defensive zone.

Derrick had just blown a great scoring opportunity.

I should have passed to her, Derrick thought, slapping his hip pad in frustration.

By the time he picked up his stick, Derrick was too far behind to make any difference in the play. He could only watch as Schonberg dodged around Sam Kruger, then pumped a perfect slap shot into the far left corner of the net. Derrick's heart sank, and he slapped his stick to the ice.

The first period wasn't even over yet, and already Schonberg had racked up two goals. The score was Williamsport 2, Alden 0.

"Hey Derrick," Chris said angrily, as they lined up at center ice for another faceoff, "I was wide open back there. You guys haven't passed to me once all game."

Chris looked like she was about to haul off and sock somebody. Derrick shrugged, then skated up to meet Schonberg for the faceoff.

The ref dropped the puck into the faceoff circle, and Derrick took a whack at Schonberg's stick. He knocked Schonberg's stick out of position, then hooked the puck off to the side. Chris fought for control of the puck with a Williamsport winger, then gained possession.

She sped down the left boards, stickhandling. Derrick had already charged across the blue line and was in perfect position for a pass, skating across empty ice.

Is she going to pass to me? Derrick wondered, as he skated toward the goal. *Or is she too angry?*

Her pass was perfect—fast and right on target. Derrick angled the blade of his stick, flicked his wrist, and watched the puck deflect into the air, flipping end over end. The Williamsport goalie leaped for it, thrusting his catcher's mitt into the air, but missed the puck by a full foot.

"Goal!" Derrick cried, as he lifted his arms.

Josh and Woody gave him a huge bear hug, and Chris skated up with a bright smile. Derrick nodded in her direction, but didn't give her a hug, a high five, or even a pat on the helmet. He almost wanted to, since Chris *had* given him the perfect assist— but still, he didn't want Coach to think Chris had become one of the guys.

When the second period ended, the score was still Williamsport 2, Alden 1. Schonberg had scored one more goal than Derrick. But in the third and final period, Derrick had plans to change that.

"I want to see some more teamwork out there in this period," Coach Campbell said, right before the

Panthers skated back onto the ice. "We missed some great passing opportunities in the first two periods. Keep your eyes open, Panthers. Remember, we're still behind by one."

Derrick won the faceoff, hooking the puck, and skated away. Chris was in perfect position for a pass, standing at the blue line. Out of the corner of his eye, Derrick saw two Williamsport defensemen speeding toward him, and decided it was time to give Chris a pass.

Chris picked up the solid pass and sped toward the goal, all alone. Derrick raced behind her to get the rebound—but it wasn't necessary. Chris did some fancy stickhandling, faked a slap shot, then scooted the puck right under the goalie's pads and into the net.

The Alden fans began to cheer and Chris lifted up her arms. It was a beautiful goal. Derrick gave Chris a little nod, then turned back around and headed toward the faceoff circle. When he got there, Josh gave him a cold glare.

"Why'd you have to make her look so good?" Josh asked under his breath.

"She was open," Derrick said with a shrug. "And we were behind."

With only twenty-two seconds left in the game, and the score still tied, Schonberg took a giant shot on goal. A.J. made a beautiful save—diving like a third baseman—and barely snagging the puck in his mitt.

"Looks like I'll be the high scorer this game," Schonberg said with a smirk, as he and Derrick squared-off for a faceoff in the Panthers' defensive zone. "And for the season, too."

Derrick didn't respond. He only stared Schonberg in the eye, then got ready for the faceoff. Once again he whacked Schonberg's stick out of the way and hooked the puck over to Woody. Derrick took off skating and Woody tipped the puck back into Derrick's stick. Derrick felt a huge smash against his side as a Williamsport player threw a body check, but he was able to pass up to Chris, who crossed the blue line in a blur.

Derrick regained his balance and raced up to help Chris, who was being blocked in by a defenseman. Derrick glanced up at the clock. There were only four seconds left in the game. He skated toward the goal, lifting his hand for a pass. Somehow, Chris wrestled free and scooped a perfect pass to Derrick. All Derrick had to do was take his stick back and smash the puck into the corner of the goal, just as the buzzer sounded.

"Yes!" Derrick shouted, raising his arms in victory.

It had been an amazing play. The Panthers had won their first game, and Derrick gave Schonberg a triumphant smile as he skated toward the locker room.

"Let's go to Pete's Pizza," Bannister said, as the boys left the locker room that evening. "We have to celebrate our first victory of the season . . . with a *lot* of pizza."

"Sounds good to me," Derrick said, slinging his gym bag over his shoulder as he walked. "I could go for something to eat."

Derrick, Josh, Woody, Bannister, Sam, and A.J. were all heading down the hall in a big group, laughing and joking. Derrick loved to win the first game of the season—it meant good luck.

Chris came out of the girl's locker room just as the boys were passing. She was wearing jeans and a sweater, just like all the guys.

"Here she is, the star play-maker of the game," Bannister said, making a dramatic gesture. "With a goal and two perfect assists."

"Where are you all headed?" Chris asked.

"We're going somewhere," Josh said shortly. "And you're not invited."

Derrick got shoved along with the group as they moved out the door. Still, he couldn't help looking back at Chris. She was standing alone with a sad expression on her face.

4

The following Sunday, Derrick was walking to Black's Pond to practice his stickhandling. He had his skates slung across his hockey stick as he cut through the snowy winter woods. The December sky was cold and blue, and the sun shone brightly on the snow—so brightly that Derrick had to squint his eyes. The pine and maple trees were covered in a blanket of white and, here and there, rabbit tracks led off through the powdery snow. As he approached

Black's Pond, Derrick took a deep breath and smiled. Winter was definitely his favorite season.

"Uh-oh," he muttered, stopping short and ducking behind a tree trunk. There was someone else on the pond, skating in graceful figure eights, and it looked like Chris Santini. Derrick was a little embarrassed by how he and his friends had been treating Chris—especially since she had played so well against Williamsport. His face turned red, and he decided to head back home so he wouldn't even have to talk to her. But after three steps, Derrick heard Chris yelling after him.

"Hey Derrick!" she shouted, cupping her hands around her mouth. "Come on down, the ice is perfect!"

Derrick let out a deep sigh and turned around. He guessed it wouldn't be that bad to work on a few plays with Chris.

"You played a great game against Williamsport," Chris said, speeding around the pond. "You know something? You don't play like the rest of the team. You play like you're from hockey country—someplace like Michigan, or Minnesota, or Canada."

Derrick couldn't help smiling. "You're right," he said, moving out onto the ice. "I'm from Minnesota."

Derrick caught up with Chris, and the two of them skated around the ice, warming up. "I moved to Cranbrook last year, right at the start of hockey season."

"Oh, just like me," Chris said.

"Yeah, I guess so," Derrick answered with a laugh. He remembered what it had been like to move to a new school in the middle of the year. He had been lonely for his old friends back in Minnesota, especially his old teammates on the state championship hockey team. It hadn't been easy at all, and he wondered if Chris was having a hard time, too. "How do you like Cranbrook so far?" Derrick asked, as they dodged through the cattails by the pond-side.

Chris shrugged her shoulders. "It's okay, I guess," she said, halfheartedly. "But I still miss my friends back in Michigan."

"I bet Michigan and Minnesota are a lot alike," Derrick said. "Really cold winters, lots of ponds and snow, and *everybody* plays hockey."

"Exactly!" Chris said. "And winter is my favorite season."

"Mine too," Derrick said with a smile.

"I love it when the weather gets really cold," Chris said. "And all the ponds freeze up, and everybody goes out to skate and play hockey. If this were Michigan or Minnesota, this pond would be jammed with people."

Derrick agreed. Still, he was glad the pond wasn't jammed with people. It was nice just to skate around, taking long smooth strides and talking. He was beginning to think that it might not be so bad to have Chris on the team.

Suddenly Chris crouched down and drove her shoulder into Derrick's chest. Surprised by the body check, Derrick tumbled to the ice and slid into a patch of reeds.

Chris let out a big laugh.

"You deserve it," she said, skating back to Derrick. "I think it's about time you guys on the team started treating me like a real player. I did give you two assists in the last game, you know."

Derrick laughed as Chris helped him back up to his skates. He had to respect *anyone* who could check like that—whether they were a boy or a girl.

"You did give me two beautiful assists," Derrick answered, wiping the ice from his sweatshirt. "And if you want to know the truth, I think you're probably a better left winger than Josh. But don't tell him I said that."

Chris smiled and then raced away. Derrick took

off after her, passed her around a corner, then knocked her to the ice with a massive hip check. Derrick could tell that Chris was a great skater—almost as good as he was—and a pretty good shooter too. But she just wasn't as strong as most of the guys on the team, and that made it easier for her to get knocked down. Derrick hoped that wouldn't cause problems for the Panthers as the season went on.

"How's that for treating you like one of the guys?" Derrick said, laughing as Chris got up slowly from the ice.

"Gee, thanks a million," Chris answered, rolling her eyes. "What about the other Panthers, like Josh? When will *they* start treating me like a member of the team?"

Derrick didn't know what to say. Derrick might have thought it was okay to have Chris on the team, but Josh was a different story. Derrick knew that Josh was still angry at having lost his position to a girl. If they could somehow convince Josh that it was okay to have Chris on the team, then the rest of the Panthers might come around, too.

"I've got an idea," Derrick said, after finishing some stickhandling drills. "The only way that Josh will accept you on the team is if he starts to like playing defense."

"Defense is great," Chris said, passing the puck to Derrick. "You get to do most of the really hard checking. And you have to skate incredibly well—backward as well as forward."

"You have to be tough, too," Derrick added, hooking the puck with his blade. "And if you're a *great* defenseman, like Bobby Orr, you can be a high scorer, too."

"Bobby Orr was the greatest!" Chris said. "One season he scored thirty-seven goals. That's pretty incredible."

"It sure is," Derrick said. "Now I have to convince *Josh* that defense can be as fun as offense."

After a few more minutes of skating, Chris said she had to head back home.

I think it's time to get to work on Josh, Derrick thought. *And I think I know exactly what to do.*

"If you think defense is so great," Josh said, "then why don't you play it yourself?"

After Derrick left Black's Pond, he hurried home to pick up a videotape and then ran over to Josh's house. The two friends walked into the family room and plopped down on the carpet, right in front of the TV. Josh's dad was sitting on the sofa with his legs crossed, smoking a pipe and reading the newspaper.

"Whose side are you on, anyway?" Josh continued. "You sound like you *want* Chris to play left wing."

"I just think you should give defense a chance," Derrick said, slipping the cassette into the VCR. "When we play North Colby next week, just try to be a great defenseman."

"What's wrong with playing defense, Josh?" Mr. Bank asked, lowering his paper and looking at the boys. "Some of the greatest players of all time were defensemen."

"But it's so boring," Josh said with a shrug.

"Boring?" Mr. Bank answered, putting his pipe down and leaning forward. "If I had to play hockey, I'd play defense for sure."

"But why?" Josh asked, looking suddenly interested.

"Because defensemen are the roughest, meanest, strongest players on the team," Mr. Bank said. "They get to do all of the really hard checking."

Derrick laughed to himself. Mr. Bank was saying everything that he had been planning to say. The difference was that Josh actually listened when his father said something.

"But they don't score goals," Josh complained.

"Oh yeah?" Mr. Bank said. "Just think about Bobby Orr, my favorite player ever. In one season alone, he scored thirty-seven goals."

"Speaking of Bobby Orr," Derrick said with a smile, pushing the play button on the VCR. "My dad has a bunch of videotapes of old NHL games. Bobby Orr is on this one."

When the picture flashed up on the TV screen, Mr. Bank sat down on the floor next to Josh.

"This is super!" Mr. Bank said. "Look at how Orr checks, digging his whole shoulder into the guy's chest. Amazing! What a great skater, too. And look! He just stole the puck."

Josh was leaning forward, watching the play with interest. Orr passed into the offensive zone, then stopped by the blue line as the forwards tried to make a play.

"See what he's doing?" Derrick said. "He's playing the point—which means that he's waiting by the blue line."

When things got jammed up in the corner, Orr got a pass on the point. He didn't hesitate for a second. He stopped the puck, lifted his stick high above his head, and slapped the puck as hard as he could.

"Great slap shot," Josh said.

The goalie fell to the ice and slid his pads to the

side, but the puck whizzed under them and into the net. Orr lifted up his stick and was mobbed by his fellow Boston Bruins.

"And who said defensemen had to be boring?" Mr. Bank asked.

Josh shrugged. "Still, it can't be as fun as winger."

"Just give it a try," Derrick said.

Mr. Bank led the boys out of the room and gave Derrick a secret wink. Derrick nodded in return— he knew that Mr. Bank was on his side. He just hoped that Josh got into playing defense in Alden's next game.

5

On Tuesday afternoon, the school bus pulled out
of Alden Junior High and turned down the road toward North Colby. Derrick was sitting in the seat
right over the wheel well, eating peanuts and listening to Josh. He glanced toward the rear of the
bus, and saw Chris sitting all by herself.

"My dad gave me a book about all the great defensemen in the NHL," Josh said to Bannister, who
was leaning over from the seat behind. "It was pretty
interesting. I'm not saying that defenseman is the

best position or anything. But you do get to give some great hip checks and body checks."

Josh paused to pop some peanuts into his mouth. "See, if the defense is good, the team will win," he continued. "You've got to remember to always have one defenseman in front of the goalie at all times. That's for extra protection. And when you steal the puck, you've got to get it out of the defensive zone as fast as you can. Then station yourself at the point, and wait for a chance to hit a giant slap shot."

"Enough talking," Bannister said. "Let's see you *play* defense." Bannister reached across their shoulders and snatched the bag of peanuts. "And don't hog all the food, either."

Derrick smiled as Josh spun around and yanked at the bag of peanuts. Derrick could tell that Josh was at least getting a little excited about his new position.

He turned around and gave Chris a secret thumbs-up.

Derrick took two long strides toward the man with the puck, then ducked his shoulder for a high body check. At the same moment, Josh skated into position on the other side of the player, and was crouching down to deliver a low hip check.

Smash! The North Colby player let out a loud grunt as he flipped over Josh's back—losing his stick and one of his gloves as he flew. He crumbled to the ice.

"Perfect!" Josh called out, as Derrick snagged the loose puck. He turned and stickhandled toward the North Colby goal.

It was already the third and final period, and neither team had scored a goal. Derrick had heard that Schonberg had scored two goals in his game the day before. That put Derrick two goals behind in the conference scoring race.

Derrick passed the puck to Chris at the blue line and followed her into the Panthers' offensive zone. He skated right down the middle of the ice, keeping his eye on the North Colby defense.

Chris charged forward along the left boards, getting poke checks from North Colby. She faked a cut toward the goal, and the defenseman lunged. Then Chris turned left, and sped toward the goal from the side. Derrick stationed himself right outside of the crease—the area in front of the net where only the goalie can stand—and waited to get a rebound.

Chris wound up and hit a slap shot. The puck zoomed between the defenseman's legs, and the goalie only had a split-second to react. The slap shot was high, and the goalie deflected it off to the side—right to where Derrick was standing.

Derrick blocked the puck with his leg, then flipped it above the goalie. The puck hit the back of the net, and Derrick lifted his stick in triumph.

Derrick skated over and gave Chris a high five. She had set up another easy goal for Derrick. At the next faceoff, the scoreboard read Alden 1, North Colby 0. But it wouldn't stay that way for long.

Derrick won the faceoff and passed the puck to Woody. Woody took the puck into the corner, where he got tied up by two North Colby players. Derrick skated up to try to break up the play and Woody pushed the puck out of the pack of players, and it slid right under the blade of Derrick's stick.

Keep your blade closer to the ice, Derrick thought angrily, as he watched a North Colby player speed up the ice with the puck.

Josh was the only Alden defenseman in position, and two North Colby players were charging in against him—two against one. Derrick hoped that Josh didn't try anything crazy.

North Colby's right winger sped in, and Josh cut as fast as possible toward the puck. The North Colby player was angling in toward the goal, and Josh met him at the faceoff circle with a crushing body check.

45

Both Josh and the North Colby player lost their balance and fell to the ice.

The puck drifted over to the other winger, who now had an easy, undefended shot against A.J. in the goal. He skated forward, faked a shot left, faked a shot right, and finally whacked a wrist shot into the high left corner of the goal.

With only thirty seconds left in the game, the score was tied.

"I can't believe I did that," Josh said as the teams got ready for the faceoff. "I should never check somebody when I'm the only defenseman in the play. It was so stupid!"

"Don't worry about it, Josh," Derrick said, skating into the faceoff circle. "Let's just put another goal on the board before the buzzer rings."

When the ref dropped the puck, Derrick and the North Colby center fought for control, cracking their sticks together like swords. Derrick hit his opponent's stick away for a split second—enough time to hook the puck and pass it out to Chris.

Chris stickhandled across the blue line and into the Panthers' offensive zone as the clock ticked down.

There were only twenty-six seconds left when the action got bogged down in the left corner, by the North Colby goal. Josh was waiting at the point, right by the blue line, in case North Colby broke away with the puck.

Chris whacked a long, hard pass back to Josh at the point.

Derrick watched as Josh stopped the pass, brought his stick back high behind his head, and smashed a wicked slap shot from the blue line. The goalie fell to the side and thrust his pads out, but the puck slipped in just beneath them for an amazing goal. The buzzer rang just as the puck hit the net, and Derrick couldn't believe his eyes.

Derrick was the first one to congratulate Josh with a huge bear hug.

"Great shot!" Derrick cried, as they skated toward the locker room. "Just like Bobby Orr!"

Derrick watched Chris skate over, and wondered how Josh would react. He was hoping that Josh would give her a high five and congratulate her on her great assist. Instead, Josh just nodded his head once in Chris's direction, then turned around to let out a giant whoop and slap Woody's hand.

"Let's ask Chris along to Pete's Pizza," Derrick said on the bus heading back home. He gave Josh a nudge in the ribs. "She did give you that great pass, you know."

47

"Chris?" Josh asked, laughing. "A girl, hanging out with the guys at Pete's? I don't think so."

"Oh, come on, Josh," Bannister said, leaning in from behind. "None of the North Colby players treated her like a girl. In fact, they all thought she was a boy."

"Who cares?" Josh answered. "She's a good player and I even admit that she's good for the team. But that doesn't mean I have to hang out with her."

Derrick just shook his head, and wondered what it would take for Josh to come around.

6

"Listen up, Panthers," Coach Campbell said, standing on the ice in front of the Panthers' bench. It was a few days later, and Alden was meeting Lincoln in the Municipal Rink. "Lincoln is a good team. They're tough, and we can expect to have a few bruises when it's all over. But we played a great game against North Colby, and we can do it again."

The whole team streamed over the boards and hit the ice skating. Derrick and Josh led the pack, skating close to the boards, speeding up when they passed behind the nets.

"Coach thinks this team is rough?" Josh asked, smiling as he pumped his arms. "Well I feel rough today, too. Real rough. If anyone gets me mad, they're in big trouble."

"You're starting to sound like a genuine defenseman," Derrick said.

"I guess so," Josh said with a smile.

Josh gave Derrick a little hip check, and Derrick hit the boards and skidded to a stop. When he got going again, Derrick was skating next to Chris and Bannister, at the tail end of the pack.

"Just a warning to everyone," Derrick said, bending his knees in a turn. "Josh sounds pretty riled up today."

"Mr. Josh Bank, Hothead of the Universe," Bannister said.

"Just what we need," Chris said.

"Really," Derrick answered. "Just what we need."

Derrick saw the Lincoln player approaching from the corner of his eye. He tried to pass the puck to Woody, but it was too late. Before he could flick his wrist, Derrick felt a shoulder smash against his side—and a second later, he was sprawled out on the ice.

He lifted his head from the ice and watched the Lincoln player skate off with the puck. He wasn't surprised to see who it was—number 38, a big kid with black hair. The Lincoln defender had been checking hard—and dirty—all during the first period. In fact, number 38 had already done time in the penalty box for charging.

Derrick gritted his teeth and skated off toward the action. He could already feel a big bruise on his hip. By the time he got down by the Panther goal, however, he had forgotten about his bruise, and was ready to steal the puck right back.

Derrick put the Lincoln player in his sights and sped forward. Just as the player was about to shoot a wrist shot toward the corner of the goal, Derrick skated in, kneeling down on one knee. The shot hit Derrick in the chest and fell to the ice. Derrick was able to swipe the puck away, clearing it up ice.

It was a beautiful piece of defense. Derrick could hear the Alden crowd cheering as Chris picked up the loose puck and sped toward the Lincoln goal. It was a fast break—just Chris against the Lincoln goalie.

Chris stickhandled the puck straight at the goal, faking left with her eyes. The goalie didn't budge and Chris cut to the right, hoping to put the puck into the high right corner of the net. The goalie shifted over with her.

When Chris had almost reached the goal line, she cut sharply to the left, across the middle of the ice, flicking a shot with the back of her blade. The goalie dived for the puck and batted it to the ice. He charged out of the goal to pounce on the puck and kill the play. But Chris had stopped fast and turned around, and she got to the puck a split second before the goalie. She flicked the puck above the sprawled goalie and into the corner of the open net for a heads-up goal. The Alden crowd went crazy, and Chris lifted up her arms.

The first period was almost over, and the score was now Alden 1, Lincoln 0.

At the faceoff, Derrick could tell that number 38 was mad. He was mad that Derrick had blocked his shot and that Chris had scored a goal. Derrick made him even madder by slapping his stick away and winning the faceoff.

Josh got Derrick's pass and fed the puck to Chris, who was waiting on the blue line. Number 38 sped as fast as he could down the ice, with Josh following right behind.

"Chris, watch out!" Josh called. "He's right behind you!"

It was too late. Number 38 slammed Chris in the side, flinging her against the boards. Chris's helmet cracked against the Plexiglas. She crumpled to the ice and lay perfectly still, her stick pointing out at a funny angle.

The referee blew his whistle and stopped the action.

Derrick had never seen such an obvious charge, and he felt his face get hot with anger. No one could cream his teammates like that.

Josh was the first one over to Chris. He knelt down beside her and asked Chris if she was Okay. Then number 38 skated by, knocking Josh down with his knee.

Josh jumped to his feet in an instant, pulling off his gloves and skating at the big Lincoln player with a furious expression.

"You shouldn't have done that!" Josh said, throwing punches at the player's face. In a second, the two of them were going at it, throwing nasty uppercuts and pulling at each other's jerseys. It was an all-out hockey brawl, and the crowd was on its feet.

Derrick skated into the middle of it—to try to break it up—but the Lincoln player slugged him in the jaw. After he shook the stars from his eyes, Derrick couldn't help fighting back. He threw a combination of one-two punches into the Lincoln player's stomach. Then the referee skated over and pulled the players apart.

"You three are out of the game!" the referee shouted angrily. "There's no fighting on this ice!"

"But this jerk here hurt one of our players," Josh yelled. "It was an obvious charge!"

"All three of you to the locker rooms, now!" the referee shouted back. "Off the ice!"

When he turned around, Derrick saw that the whole team was grouped around Chris. Coach bent down, put one arm around Chris and lifted her from the ice.

"She's okay," Coach said to the team. "Just shaken up. But she won't be back in this game."

Derrick and Josh silently followed Coach and Chris down the hallway that led to the locker rooms.

"Well, *that* was quite a play," Coach Campbell said, putting his hands on his hips. "In one fell swoop, we lost three of our best players. This is just fabulous."

Coach stood in the hallway near the locker rooms, shaking his head. Chris was slumped in a chair, trying to catch her breath, and Derrick and Josh were sitting on the floor beside her.

"Now Chris," Coach said, "any player who gets that shaken up has to sit out the game. No matter how important they are to the team." Coach turned to Derrick and Josh. "As for you two, haven't I told the team a hundred times—no fighting?"

"But Coach," Josh started, "that jerk . . ."

"No buts," Coach said, turning around to leave. "You can just sit here for the rest of the game and think about whether it was worth getting ejected."

Coach closed the door behind him, and the three teammates were left alone in the hallway.

"No matter what Coach says," Chris began, taking her helmet off and looking at Josh, "thanks for sticking up for me out there."

Josh shrugged. "I guess I don't like it when someone beats up on my teammates—whether they're girls or boys."

Chris smiled, and so did Derrick. It sounded like Josh was getting used to Chris being a Panther.

"That was a nice goal you made out there," Josh continued. "You've got a pretty good wrist shot."

"Thanks," Chris answered. "You played a great

game, too. That is, until you turned into Mike Tyson."

Josh laughed and pretended to punch Chris in the stomach. Chris smiled.

As the game went on, each one of the Panthers popped their head around the door to see how Chris was feeling. Bannister, Sam, John, Dave, Jack, Woody—they all wanted to make sure their star left winger was okay. Unfortunately, the news from the rink wasn't good. By the third period, the Panthers were down 3–1.

"I guess the team really needs the three of us," Josh said.

"I guess so," Derrick answered.

"You know, it's funny," Chris said. "We may be losing, and I may have bruises all over—but right now I feel better than I have all season."

"Really?" Derrick asked, confused.

"Yeah," Chris answered. "I guess I'm starting to like Cranbrook. And for the first time, I feel like a *real* member of the team."

"Watch out," Josh laughed, rolling his eyes. "You're starting to sound like a girl."

"But I am a girl," Chris said, smiling as she threw a solid punch to Josh's shoulder.

The Panthers ended up losing to Lincoln, 4–1. But after the game, the whole team—including Chris—went to Pete's Pizza. As they each stuffed their faces with pepperoni pizza, they decided they weren't going to lose another game.

7

The next week, Derrick was eating lunch with Chris, Josh, and Woody. The cafeteria of Alden Junior High was loud with the sounds of talking and the clanking of trays on tabletops. Usually, Chris sat with a bunch of girls at a table by the big plate-glass windows. But for the last few days, she'd been eating with the guys on the hockey team.

"Hey, Chris," Derrick said, tossing a handful of raisins into his mouth. "What do your friends think about you being on the hockey team?"

"Oh, they think it's great," Chris answered. "Haven't you seen them? They're at every game, cheering the whole team on."

"Oh, we've seen them, all right," Josh said, laughing. "When they scream, I bet you can hear them all the way to Williamsport. They sound like a bunch of monkeys or hyenas or something."

Chris threw a cheese curl at Josh, hitting him in the forehead. Derrick looked at Josh and smiled to himself. It had taken a while, but Derrick's plan had worked. Josh was psyched about being a defenseman, and everyone was psyched to have Chris on the team.

"Do you know what my friends tell me, though?" Chris asked, looking serious. "They tell me that I look like a boy when I'm on the ice, with my helmet on and everything. And they tell me that the other team *definitely* thinks I'm a boy."

"Your friends are probably right," Derrick said. "But who cares?"

"*I* care!" Chris cried, slapping the table with her palm. "Because I'm *not* a boy."

"But you play like a boy," Josh said, throwing a cheese curl up into the air and catching it in his mouth.

"Still, I've made a decision," Chris said, standing

59

up from the table. All the boys stopped chewing and looked up at her. "From now on I want everyone on the other team—and everyone in the stands—to know that I'm a girl. Period."

"How are you going to do that?" Woody asked.

"Before the game against St. Stephen's today," Chris began, crumpling up her lunch bag, "I'm going to skate over to the scorekeeper and tell him my full name—Christina Mary Santini. And I'll tell him to announce me using my full name. That way everyone will know I'm a girl."

Chris got up with her wadded-up bag in her hand. She turned toward a garbage can and shot her bag through the air. The bag flew high, then arced down into the garbage can and landed with a thunk. Her teammates started applauding and whistling, and Chris turned her head around and gave them all a bright smile.

"She even shoots baskets like a boy," Josh said.

Derrick watched Chris leave the lunchroom and join a group of her friends by the water fountain. He could understand how Chris felt. *He* wouldn't want people thinking that *he* was a girl. Still, he hoped that Chris's decision wouldn't cause any problems for the Panthers.

———

Derrick had his eye on the faces of the St. Stephen's players. Both teams were sitting on their benches in full uniform, listening to the lineups. The announcer's voice rang out loud, echoing throughout the big St. Stephen's rink.

"And starting for the Panthers—Derrick Larson at center, A.J. Pape at goalie, Woody Franklin at right wing, Sam Kruger and Josh Bank at defenseman, and . . . and . . . Christina Mary Santini at left wing."

Derrick saw the jaws of the whole St. Stephen's squad nearly drop to the floor. They looked over to the Panthers' bench, trying to pick out the girl. Derrick laughed to himself and climbed over the boards for the faceoff.

As Derrick skated up to the faceoff circle, he could tell that the St. Stephen's team was confused by the news that there was a girl on the ice. He won the faceoff with no problem, slapping the center's stick away and swiping the puck out to Woody.

Woody broke toward the blue line, digging his blades into the ice and stickhandling. Chris waited for Woody to cross the blue line first—so the Panthers wouldn't be offsides—and then skated forward along the left boards.

As soon as Woody crossed the line, the St. Stephen's defense was all over him, poke checking and driving him toward the boards. Derrick skated over to help, and Woody was able to get off a soft pass before he was smashed against the Plexiglas. Derrick hooked in the pass with his stick, turned, and skated toward the goal.

A St. Stephen's player charged forward, skating at full speed. Derrick lifted his stick for a slap shot, trying to smash the puck into the net before the defenseman hit him. He whipped his stick around and felt it whack the puck. The goalie made a dive to the right, but the shot never got that far. The defenseman lifted up his stick and deflected the speeding puck off to the left boards.

Chris picked up the loose puck, and cut in toward the middle. Two St. Stephen's players were there to meet her, and Derrick waited for them to check her into the boards.

But they didn't even touch her. They only skated backward, making weak little poke checks and giving Chris all the room she needed to charge the goal.

What's going on? Derrick thought, as he raced over to help Chris. *Why aren't they checking her?*

One of the St. Stephen's players backed all the way into the side of the net and tripped. In the confusion, Chris lifted her stick and hit a wrist shot, flicking the puck high into the corner of the goal.

"Yes!" Derrick shouted, giving Chris a high five. "You had those guys totally psyched out."

As Derrick skated back toward center ice, the St. Stephen's forward swept in and skated alongside him. The center's face was red, and he looked mad.

"It's a pretty cheap trick," the center said. "You put a girl on the ice so the other team can't play rough."

Derrick gave the player a stern look in the eye. "You guys don't need to treat Chris any differently."

"We're not going to cream a girl into the boards," the center replied angrily. "If we did, we'd probably kill her, or something."

Derrick turned away without giving an answer. He didn't have time to worry about St. Stephen's. If they wanted to play soft on Chris, that was all right with him—all it did was give the Panthers a huge advantage.

A few seconds later, Josh checked the St. Stephen's left winger into the boards and passed the puck up ice to Chris. The puck hit her blade right as she crossed the blue line, and Chris stickhandled into St. Stephen's territory.

Derrick kept his eye on the puck, as he skated

toward the action. Chris faked and dodged around her defenseman, who didn't even try to stop her.

Derrick shook his head. If they wanted to give Chris free reign, it would just mean more goals for him, and for the Panthers. When Chris lifted her stick to whack a slap shot, Derrick cut toward the goal to get the rebound.

The shot was a little high, and the St. Stephen's goalie knocked it down with his glove. Derrick was right there, speeding in toward the crease with his eyes focused on the loose puck. He scooped the puck away, turned around, and flipped the puck into the corner for a goal.

For the rest of the game, the Panthers ruled the ice. St. Stephen's was usually a good team, but they just seemed to crumble. In the second period, Chris scored a goal, Josh scored a goal, and Derrick scored two—for his first hat trick of the season. In the third period, Woody scored one, and Sam Kruger whacked in a slap shot from the point. The final score was Alden 8, St. Stephen's 1.

When Bannister rushed into Pete's Pizza later that afternoon, all the food was gone. Derrick, Chris, Josh, Woody, Sam, and A.J. were sitting at a big round table, with three empty pans in front of them.

"Where's the pizza?" Bannister cried, his eyes opening wide.

Everyone shrugged their shoulders and patted their stomachs.

"Since you guys are such pigs, I won't tell you the news I heard," Bannister said, crossing his arms stubbornly.

"What news?" Derrick asked, leaning forward. "Did you hear about how Williamsport did in their game today?"

Williamsport was Alden's biggest competitor for the conference championship—not to mention that it was also Schonberg's team. If Williamsport won their game, they would be solidly in first place. If they lost, they'd be tied for first with Alden.

Just then, another large pepperoni pizza arrived at the table, and Bannister broke into a smile. He sat down and grabbed a huge slice.

"Williamsport *lost* today," he said before taking a gigantic bite. He chewed fast, swallowed, and looked over to Derrick. "And for *your* information, Schonberg scored two goals. That means you're tied with him for first place in conference scoring."

"One thing's for sure," Chris said. "Williamsport won't be in first place after we play them on Tuesday."

"And Schonberg won't be in first place for scoring, either," Derrick said with confidence.

8

That Sunday, Derrick and Chris met on Black's Pond to work on stickhandling and passing. It was a very cold day, and the sky was gray and windy. As they skated up and down the ice, whacking passes back and forth, their faces and ears turned bright red with cold. Soon, snow began to swirl down, spinning like confetti in the brisk wind.

"I wish we got more snow in Cranbrook," Derrick said, pushing a pass to Chris. Derrick's face was so cold that his lips hardly moved when he talked. "It's

67

not like living up north, in Michigan or Minnesota."

"But it does get cold enough in Cranbrook," Chris said, hooking the pass and stickhandling the puck up ice. "And speaking of cold, let's take a break. I brought some hot chocolate in a Thermos."

That sounded great to Derrick. They skated into the reeds and sat down on a log by the shore. Chris unscrewed the top from her Thermos bottle, and billows of thick steam rose up in the cold air. She poured Derrick a big cupful, laughing when she dumped some on his skate by accident. Derrick warmed his hands on the cup, and sipped the hot chocolate.

They sat for a while, not saying anything at all—just watching the snow fall and the steam rise up from their cups.

"Are you ready for the big game on Tuesday?" Chris asked after a while. "Williamsport is going to come out fighting, for sure."

"We can take them," Derrick answered. "We beat them earlier this season, and we can beat them again." Derrick took a sip of hot chocolate. "Besides, I think we've gotten better since then. You and Woody and I work really well as a front line. And if we keep practicing hard, we'll just keep getting better."

"What about Schonberg?" Chris asked. "He's been playing pretty well recently, too."

"Oh, well," Derrick said with a shrug. "As long as the team wins, that's the important thing. If I beat Schonberg in scoring, that's just icing on the cake."

Derrick knew he wasn't quite telling the whole truth. He did want the Panthers to have a good season. But he wanted to win the high-scoring trophy every bit as much—and maybe more.

"Besides," Derrick continued, "as long as you and Woody are on the ice, I'll do great. And so will the Panthers."

That Monday, when Derrick hit the ice at practice, he noticed a man in a green-and-white cap standing next to Coach Campbell. Derrick was sure that he'd seen the man before, but he couldn't remember where. Whoever he was, he was making Coach Campbell look very concerned.

When the Panthers were ready to start practice, Coach blew his whistle and the team gathered at the boards.

"I'd like you all to meet someone," Coach said, nodding to the man in the green-and-white cap. "This is Coach Blakey, the coach of the Williamsport team."

Now Derrick remembered the man. He should have known anyway, since green and white were the Williamsport colors. But what was the Williamsport coach doing here?

"Coach Blakey is the chairman of the Conference Rules Committee," Coach Campbell went on, looking very serious. "If anyone has a complaint about a game, they take it to the Rules Committee, and the committee makes the final decision."

Derrick was starting to get a bad feeling in the pit of his stomach. He looked over to Chris, and Chris shrugged.

"Last week, the St. Stephen's coach filed a complaint," Coach continued. "Our victory against St. Stephen's has been contested. The coach thinks that it's illegal to have a girl on the team, and that we should forfeit the game."

Derrick's mouth dropped open. He looked over at Chris, and Chris was shaking her head in disbelief.

"I'm in charge of making the ruling," the Williamsport coach said, taking off his cap. "So I'm here today not as the Williamsport coach, but as the chairman of the Conference Rules Committee."

"Yeah, right," Josh said to Derrick under his breath. "I bet that guy does everything he can to make sure Williamsport wins the game tomorrow."

Derrick hoped that Josh was wrong. Coach Campbell told the team to work on their shooting drills, and Derrick, Woody, and Chris skated to the blue line. Josh and Sam got in their defensive positions, and A.J. crouched down in the goal.

The drill was simple—the offense tried to score.

Chris skated forward, then passed left to Derrick. Sam rushed at Derrick, but Derrick dodged around him and whacked a slap shot right at the goal. It deflected off the goal post and flew up high into the air, spinning end over end. Derrick skated toward the puck, choked up on his stick and brought it back like a baseball bat. He took a swipe at the falling puck and batted it right into the corner of the goal.

The whole team went crazy, laughing and clapping. No one had ever seen a play like that, and Derrick skated back to the blue line with a smile.

When Derrick looked over to the bench, he noticed that the Williamsport coach was heading out the door. Coach Campbell blew his whistle and the team skated up to him.

"Bad news," Coach said, looking depressed. "Chris has been suspended from play until the committee can make an official ruling."

"What?" several Panthers cried. "Suspended?"

Chris didn't say a thing. She just stood there, staring blankly at the ice.

"Coach Blakey is pretty sure that it's illegal for a girl to play in this conference," Coach went on. "It seems the football rules were updated, but not the ones for hockey. We won't know anything until the committee has its monthly meeting. And that's not until Wednesday."

"Wednesday?" Derrick asked. "But we play Williamsport tomorrow. And we need Chris on the ice."

"I wish she could play, too," Coach said. "But the rules are the rules. She'll have to sit out until we get a final ruling."

"That coach just wants his team to win tomorrow," Josh said. "It's so obvious."

"That's enough!" Coach said sharply. "Now let's get back to practice everyone—except Chris. We've got a big game tomorrow."

Derrick could hardly believe what had just happened. Suddenly, Chris wasn't able to play, just because she was a girl.

Didn't they understand? Chris wasn't just a girl— she was a *Panther*.

"I'm sorry about this, guys," Chris said as the team

skated back out to center ice. "I hope I didn't ruin the whole season."

"No way," Derrick answered, slapping his stick against the ice. "We're going to fight this to the end." He looked around at his teammates. "Aren't we, guys?"

"Yeah!" everyone shouted.

9

Derrick's shoulder hit the Plexiglas first, and then his whole body swung around and smashed into the boards. He could feel Schonberg's hip and elbow driving into his back, as he fought to keep control of the puck. From the corner of his eye, Derrick could see the Williamsport fans slapping the Plexiglas, trying to distract him.

"Too bad you guys lost your star left winger," Schonberg muttered, as he tried to dig the puck out with his stick.

"I'm still going to win the scoring title, Schonberg," Derrick answered, trying to kill the puck by trapping it against the boards with his skate.

Schonberg rammed Derrick hard against the boards. "How come you guys aren't wearing pretty pink bows in your hair?" he said. "You're sure *playing* like a bunch of girls."

Schonberg suddenly hooked the puck away and skated up ice. Derrick turned angrily and sped toward the action.

Alden and Williamsport were playing in the Williamsport Municipal Rink. As Derrick skated after Schonberg, charging across the blue line toward the Panthers' goal, he glanced into the stands and caught a glimpse of Chris. She was sitting all alone, in her everyday clothes, watching the game with a sad expression. Derrick couldn't believe how much he, and the rest of the team, missed her on the ice. She made a lot of the big plays happen—and so far, the Panthers hadn't made *any* big plays at all. The first period was almost over, and the score was already Williamsport 2, Alden 0.

Derrick watched Schonberg pass off to his left winger, and then saw Bannister charge in for a check. Bannister looked funny, like the Goodyear Blimp on skates, as he crouched down to deliver a hip check to the Williamsport left winger. Since Chris was off the ice, Josh had been moved up to left winger, and Bannister had replaced Josh as first-team defenseman.

The new lineup was turning out to be a disaster.

The Williamsport left winger cut to the side, a quick slice and turn on his skates, and Bannister barrelled past him and crashed into the boards. Derrick raced over, and the winger passed the puck past Derrick to a defenseman, who was waiting at the point. The defenseman lifted his stick and took a slap shot, which missed the goal and hit the Plexiglas in the right corner. Schonberg picked up the puck, faked out Sam with a head fake, and cut across the front of the goal.

Derrick charged forward, but he was too late. He could only watch as Schonberg slipped the puck into the goal, right under A.J.'s pads.

"I can't believe it," Derrick said to Josh, as they skated back for the faceoff. "Schonberg has already scored two goals today. It's enough to make me want to punch him in the face."

"Let's not get into another fight," Josh said, stopping at the faceoff circle.

Derrick had to laugh. Suddenly Josh—of all people—was trying to calm Derrick down, when usually it was just the other way around. That wasn't a very good sign. Just before the faceoff, Derrick looked up to Chris in the stands. Chris gave him a thumbs-up, but it didn't lift Derrick's spirits at all.

Schonberg won the faceoff and passed to his winger. As the winger turned to skate, Sam hip checked him and slapped the puck to Josh. Once Josh cleared the blue line, Derrick took off toward the Williamsport goal.

I need to score a goal, Derrick thought, looking for a pass from Josh. It was a perfect scoring situation.

Josh was in trouble against the left boards, blocked in by the Williamsport defenseman. He tried to pass the puck in to Derrick, who was speeding toward the goal, but the pass was way off target. Schonberg put his stick out, intercepted the pass, then turned and skated up ice—stealing Alden's best chance to score.

When the buzzer sounded to end the first period, Derrick shook his head and skated slowly toward the bench. He knew that Chris would have made the pass. Suddenly, he got the sinking feeling that the Panthers' season was in trouble—not to mention his hopes of beating Schonberg for the scoring trophy.

"Listen up, men," Coach Campbell said in the locker room. "We need to get back on our feet. We don't look like the Alden Panthers out there. I know we're missing one of our best players, but we've got to make up for it."

"But every time I look over at that Williamsport coach," Josh said, "all I can think is that he suspended Chris just so his team could have an advantage today."

"Coach Blakey is just doing his job," Coach answered. "And it's about time you guys started doing yours. Next period, I want to see some of the old Panther spirit. We can beat these guys. Now let's do it!"

The second period started off well for the Panthers. Two minutes after the faceoff, Josh poke checked Schonberg, knocking the puck away. Josh skated around Schonberg in a flash, recovering the loose puck and looking for an opening to pass. He whacked the puck up to Derrick, who skated across the blue line, getting heavy coverage from a defenseman. Derrick head-faked to the left, then slapped a sharp pass to the right, where Woody was skating all alone.

Derrick felt his winning spirit come back as he watched Woody charge the net. A Williamsport defenseman was waiting for Woody, shielding the goal. Woody hesitated and feinted right, drawing the defenseman forward. At the right second, Woody poked his stick around the defenseman and flicked the puck high into the corner of the goal, just beyond the reach of the Williamsport goaltender.

Woody's goal brought the score to Williamsport 2, Alden 1. But it didn't stay that way for long.

Four minutes into the second period, Derrick felt the Panthers' spirit start to fade again. He was stick-handling up ice when Schonberg swooped in from behind and picked the puck off. Derrick could hardly believe it—he felt like he'd just *handed* the puck to Schonberg.

Schonberg turned quickly and sped toward the Panther goal. Sam and Bannister were waiting to meet him, but Schonberg didn't give them a chance. He slowed down, lifted his stick high above his shoulders, and hit a slap shot so hard that Bannister turned and hid his face. The puck rocketed into the corner of the net, and A.J. ended up in a heap, face down on the ice.

"Gee," Schonberg said to Derrick, as they waited for the ref to skate to the faceoff circle, "I guess the Panthers' whole game depends on a *girl*. Why don't you guys just forfeit?" Schonberg turned around and let out a loud laugh, and the other Williamsport players laughed along.

"A bunch of sissies, that's what the Panthers are," one Williamsport player said.

"I wouldn't be surprised if they're all girls," another one commented.

Derrick felt his blood begin to boil. He skated up to Schonberg, and was about to throw his gloves down and give Schonberg a punch in the face. But the ref skated between them and told everyone to chill out. Derrick tried to concentrate on playing hockey, but he was so mad he could hardly even see straight.

Williamsport ended up winning the game 5–1. Schonberg scored three goals—a hat-trick—and Derrick ended the day without so much as a single assist.

"What a lousy game," Derrick said. He slumped down into his seat and crossed his arms over his chest.

The Panthers were on the bus, heading home from Williamsport. Derrick and Josh were sitting together and Chris and Bannister sat behind them. The team was quiet and still. There was none of the noise and laughter that filled the bus when the Panthers were victorious.

"I'm worried about that Conference Rules Committee meeting tomorrow night," Chris said. "What do you guys think the committee is going to decide?"

"They could decide anything," Bannister answered. "If it's really illegal for a girl to play on the team, then they might even make us forfeit the whole season."

"The whole season?" Josh cried. "No way!"

"Yes way," Bannister said. "Those are the rules."

"Oh, that's just *great* news," Chris said, rolling her eyes.

Hearing that made Derrick more depressed than ever. He had had big plans for this season. Now, suddenly, it looked like he might end up without a season at all.

"Sorry, guys," Chris said. "It looks like I really screwed things up."

"Maybe there's something we can do," Derrick said.

"Like what?" Josh asked. "The meeting is tomorrow night."

"I don't know what," Derrick said, shaking his head. "Just give me a little time. I'll think of something."

———

Derrick was watching TV when the idea came to him. He leaped up from the sofa, knocking down a glass of orange juice that he'd put on the coffee table.

"Derrick!" Mrs. Larson said. "What's the matter?"

"I figured it out!" Derrick said, ignoring the spilled juice. His mind was working at a thousand miles per hour. "I figured out what to do!"

"What to do about what?" Mrs. Larson said, hurrying into the kitchen to get some paper towels.

"About Chris," Derrick answered. "Do you see all the people on the news right there?" Derrick pointed at the TV screen, which showed a group of protesters marching around in front of a government building. They held up big painted signs and were chanting slogans. "Do you see what they're doing?"

"Of course I do, Derrick," Mrs. Larson answered, handing Derrick a pile of paper towels. "They're trying to tell the government what they think. And I'm telling *you* to clean up your mess."

Derrick was smiling as he knelt down and cleaned up the spilled juice. It was so simple. The Panthers would get together and paint signs. They'd call the Cranbrook TV station and tell them that they were staging a demonstration. Then they'd all go to the meeting of the Conference Rules Committee and march around, carrying signs and yelling cheers.

That way the committee—and everyone who was watching TV—would know that the Panthers were backing Chris 100 percent.

If they were lucky, they might even convince the committee to let Chris stay on the team, and finish the season as an Alden Panther.

Suddenly Derrick felt all his energy come back. If the Panthers were going to stage a demonstration tomorrow night, they'd have to get to work right now.

Derrick asked his parents if the whole team could come over that night, to paint signs and make plans. When they said okay, Derrick rushed to the phone and called each and every player on the team.

"We've got to get together tonight and make signs," he told them. "Let's convince the committee that Chris is a real Panther."

Everyone met at Derrick's after dinner. While Josh and Alex got started making signs, Bannister and Woody and Sam and John began painting a huge banner, made from an old sheet. As soon as Derrick saw that everyone was busy, he left the room to make a phone call.

"Who did you say you were calling?" Chris asked Derrick. She followed him into the Larsons' kitchen.

"The local TV station," Derrick said, picking up the phone.

"No way!" Chris said, turning red. "I'd be so embarrassed if I had to go on TV."

"Too bad," Derrick said, punching the numbers. "We want you to stay a Panther, and we're going to do everything we can to make sure you do."

10

"Let's get this banner up fast," Derrick said the next night, scrambling up a ladder outside Williamsport Junior High. "Josh, grab the other end. Sam, hand me the tape."

The Panthers were in a flurry of activity—testing the megaphone, painting last minute signs, hanging banners above the doors to the meeting room. It was a freezing night, with bright stars in the black sky, but everyone was too busy to feel cold.

"Lift your end of the banner a little higher," Derrick called out to Josh. "There! Perfect!"

Derrick climbed down off the ladder and looked up at the banner with a smile. The banner read, in blue and gold letters, KEEP CHRIS A PANTHER!

"Looks good, guys," Derrick said, turning around and pacing off toward the rest of the team. "Now everyone grab your signs. The members of the committee will be showing up soon."

"And so will the TV news crew," Josh added.

Coach Campbell was the first to arrive. He was going to make a big speech to the committee, explaining why Chris should be allowed to play. Earlier that day, Derrick had read the official conference rules. The rules *did* use the word "boy" all the time, and never mentioned girls. Still, the rules were written in 1953, and things had changed since then. Nowadays, girls could do anything that boys could— and it was Coach's job to convince the committee of that.

Coach broke into a big smile when he saw the whole team together, holding signs that said WE'RE BEHIND CHRIS! and GIVE GIRLS A CHANCE! and LET CHRIS PLAY! Coach thought it was a great idea for the team to show its support for Chris—as long as things didn't get out of hand.

"Just keep your heads screwed on straight," Coach said with a smile, as he walked past the team and into the meeting room.

Just then, the truck from Cranbrook TV News pulled into the parking lot. That's when Bannister grabbed a megaphone, put it up to his mouth, and started shouting, "Keep Chris a Panther! Keep Chris a Panther! Keep Chris a Panther!"

The whole team joined in—except Chris, who just looked embarrassed. By the time the TV camera was set up, the Panthers were marching around in a big circle, bobbing their signs up and down, and chanting loudly.

The reporter pulled Chris and Derrick out of the group to hold an interview. Derrick felt his heart pound like crazy as he looked into the bright lights and the camera.

"I'm standing here with Chris Santini and Derrick Larson," the reporter began, holding a microphone. "Chris is a girl, and the Conference Rules Committee is meeting here tonight to decide if she's allowed to continue playing hockey with the boys." With that he turned to Chris. "Chris, how do you feel right now?" he said, holding the microphone up to her.

"I feel scared," Chris answered. "I just want to play

hockey with my friends. I don't think it should matter if I'm a girl or a boy."

"And how have your teammates treated you?" he asked.

"Well, at first they were kind of mad to have a girl on the team," Chris said. "But now they think I'm okay."

The whole team let out a big cheer behind her.

"And next to Chris is Derrick Larson, the boy who put this whole demonstration together," the reporter said, turning to Derrick. Derrick felt beads of cold sweat break out on his forehead, and he swallowed hard. "Derrick, why did you go through the trouble of putting this together? Do you really want to have a girl on your team?"

"Chris is a great hockey player," Derrick began. "She may be a girl, but that doesn't matter to us— and it shouldn't matter to the Rules Committee, either. The Alden Panthers are behind Chris all the way."

A moment later, the lights went out and the camera stopped rolling. The reporter thanked Chris and Derrick and sent them back to the group.

"You're TV stars!" Bannister cried. "Can I have your autographs, please?"

"Very funny," Derrick said with a smile, picking

up his sign and joining the march. "How did I sound when I talked?"

"Just like Peter Jennings," Bannister said.

A few minutes later, the Williamsport coach got out of his car, looking very confused. He walked as fast as he could toward the meeting room, without even looking at the banners or the signs.

"Keep Chris a Panther! Keep Chris a Panther!" everyone shouted at him as he opened up the door and disappeared inside.

When all the members of the committee had gone into the meeting, the news truck packed up, tooted its horn, and rolled away. No one was in the parking lot but the Panthers, and the night was suddenly quiet. Everyone sat down on their signs and poured cups of hot chocolate.

"I wish we could hear what they're saying in there," Derrick said. "I bet Coach Campbell is really giving it to them."

"I hope so," Chris answered, sighing. "If we have to forfeit this whole season because of me, I don't know what I'll do."

"Don't worry about it," Josh answered. "You're a Panther, and that's that."

Derrick saw the door open, and a group of boys walked out. It was dark, and Derrick couldn't tell who they were until they were close by. As soon as he recognized them, Derrick felt his face turn red.

It was Schonberg, and a few guys from the Williamsport team.

"Well, if it isn't the sissies!" Schonberg said, stopping and looking at the team. "Sticking up for your girlfriend?"

Derrick may not have liked Schonberg very much, but he had to admire his guts. The Williamsport boys were outnumbered two to one.

"We'll meet you in the championship," Derrick said, stepping forward and standing right in front of Schonberg. "And then we'll see who gets the last laugh."

"You guys aren't even going to get to play another game," Schonberg said. "Our coach says that you'll have to forfeit the whole season for breaking conference rules."

"But the rules were written in 1953," Derrick said. "Things are different now."

"One thing hasn't changed," Schonberg said, pushing Derrick once in the chest. "*If* we meet you on the ice again, we're still going to cream you."

Derrick pushed Schonberg back, but Josh and Woody broke them up before they could throw any punches.

"Just wait until you hear what the committee decides," Schonberg shouted, as he headed down the street. "Then we'll see who gets the last laugh!"

The meeting seemed to go on forever. Standing in the cold, Derrick wondered what the committee could be talking about for so long. Some of the Panthers had started to whisper that Chris was probably going to be suspended—and that the team would have to forfeit its whole season. Derrick tried to keep the Panthers in high spirits, but it wasn't easy to do.

The night got colder and colder. Everyone was stamping their feet and blowing into their hands to keep warm. Derrick walked over to where Chris and Josh were standing, and poured himself a cup of hot chocolate.

"You know what I think?" Derrick said, sipping from the steaming cup. "I don't think they're going to come up with a final decision tonight."

"Oh, I hope they do," Chris answered. "I can't keep waiting and waiting."

"Besides, we have a game the day after tomorrow," Josh said. "They've got to make a decision before that."

The door finally opened and the committee members began to walk out. The whole team jumped to attention, and rushed over to Coach Campbell. Coach stopped, shoved his hands into his coat pockets, and gave his team a little smile.

"Well, Panthers," Coach said. "The committee has not come up with a final decision."

Everyone moaned.

"But wait," Coach said, lifting up his hand. "I told them exactly how we feel. I told them that Chris has the same right as anyone else to play hockey. I pointed out that if girls can play football, then they can play hockey, too."

The team let out a cheer.

"But the Williamsport coach said that we broke the conference rules," Coach continued. "He said that we should have to forfeit our whole season."

The team was silent.

"The committee said that they need to think about it longer," Coach went on. "They said they would call me with a ruling before the next game—which is in two days." Coach lifted the collar up on his coat, to block the cold wind. "Now, it's time we all got some sleep. We have a big practice tomorrow. I called Mrs. Larson and Mrs. Bank, and the car pool is on its way to pick you up and take you home."

The team picked up all the signs, took down the banners, and walked toward the parking lot. Derrick could see his mother's car pulling into the drive. He knew that the team had done everything it could to help Chris. Now all they could do was wait.

11

It was the next afternoon, and the Panthers were at practice in the Cranbrook Municipal Rink. Derrick stickhandled the puck past the blue line, keeping Josh in the corner of his eye. Sam Kruger and Bannister were on defense, and Sam skated out to meet Derrick near the right faceoff circle. Derrick lifted his stick for a slap shot, but Sam got his stick on the puck just as Derrick swung his arms through. The two sticks cracked together, making a sound like a gunshot, and the puck went skipping off to the side.

I can't believe it, Derrick thought, as he cut toward the puck. *I haven't played so badly in years.*

The whole team was in a bad mood, and so far, practice had been sloppy. If they were going to have to forfeit the whole season tomorrow, Derrick wondered why they should practice hard today.

Derrick skated after the loose puck, hooked it with his stick, and looked for Josh. Josh had skated around the back of the net, and was speeding up the right boards. Derrick flicked him a pass with the back of his stick, and Josh picked it up near the faceoff circle.

Bannister skated forward, cutting off Josh's angle on the goal. Josh tried to dodge around Bannister, but Bannister gave him a hip check and sent him flying to the ice. Sam picked up the loose puck and stickhandled it up ice.

Coach blew his whistle.

"You guys are looking pretty bad out there," Coach said, as Derrick and Josh skated back into the line at center ice. "Josh, you didn't keep your head up. You looked down at the puck when you were stickhandling. That gave Bannister the chance to take you out of the play."

Derrick watched as the next two Panthers charged forward toward the goal. He just didn't feel like playing hockey.

"Can you believe that Bannister took me out?" Josh asked, shaking his head.

"I just hope Coach gets the news soon," Derrick said.

On Derrick's next turn, he decided he was going to score a goal no matter what. Josh started off with the puck, skating down the left boards. Before Bannister had a chance to check him, Josh whacked a slap shot on goal. A.J. blocked it easily, deflecting the puck off to the side. Derrick raced after the loose puck, pumping his hips as he picked up speed. Sam beat him to the puck, however, and swept it across the ice to Bannister.

But Derrick didn't slow down. He picked up speed as he raced behind the net, crossing one skate over the other and bending his knees. Bannister was stickhandling slowly up ice and Derrick zoomed in from behind, snatching the puck off of Bannister's stick. Derrick felt his heart begin to pound as he turned toward the goal and lifted his stick. He wanted to make this shot—just to prove that he could ignore the Panthers' bad mood and still be the star of the team.

He slapped the puck as hard as he could, and watched it take off toward the goal. Suddenly the puck curved way off target, lifting over the Plexiglas and flying high into the empty stands. He had missed by a mile, and he shook his head as he skated back into line.

"Okay, men," Coach called out, stepping onto the ice. "That's it for practice. Gather around."

Derrick skated slowly over to the side, with his head down. Chris was sitting right behind Coach, watching everything happen on the ice.

"As you all know, I haven't heard a thing from the Conference Rules Committee," Coach began. "But we have to practice like we're going to be in the championship. Right?"

The team shrugged and nodded.

"We have a game tomorrow, against South Colby," Coach went on. "If we lose, we don't have any chance of making it to the conference championship. I know that everyone wants Chris to be out on the ice. But until we hear from the committee, she can't play. Period. The rest of us have to go out there tomorrow and show South Colby what the Panthers are really made of."

"Coach?" Chris asked, standing up from the bench. "Can I say something?"

"Sure, Chris," Coach said.

Chris took a deep breath and began. "I just want to thank everyone on the team. I'm very happy and proud to be an Alden Panther. And I only hope that the team doesn't have to forfeit the whole season."

Derrick and the rest of the team waited for Chris to say more. But Chris just turned and ran out the door toward the locker rooms.

"Where's Chris?" Woody asked, as the boys walked out of the locker room a few minutes later. "Isn't she going to come with us to the Game Place?"

"She's usually waiting right here for us," Derrick said.

Derrick looked around the hallway, knocked on the girls' locker room door, and called into the empty rink—but there was no answer.

"She probably went home," Bannister said, as the boys walked out into the cold evening. "She seemed pretty upset that she wrecked our whole season, not to mention wrecking Derrick's chances to win the high-scoring trophy."

Derrick thought it was strange. Chris, with her great passing, had been a big reason why Derrick stood a chance of beating Schonberg for the scoring trophy. Now, Chris might also be the one who ruined his chances of taking the trophy home.

The boys walked over to the Cranbrook Mall and into the Game Place. They all bought sodas and walked back to their favorite knob hockey table. Nobody felt much like playing, and after standing around for a few minutes, talking about the Panthers' strange season, they all decided just to head home.

12

"I got a call today from the Conference Rules Committee," Coach Campbell said the next afternoon. He was standing on the ice in the Cranbrook Municipal Rink, talking to all the players seated on the bench. Everyone was in their blue-and-gold hockey uniforms—except Chris, who sat next to Derrick wearing an Alden sweatshirt. Derrick glanced at Chris, and gave her a little smile. He hoped that Coach Campbell had good news.

Coach cleared his voice and continued talking.

"They said they haven't reached a final decision yet."

"What?" Derrick cried. "We're about to start the game!"

"I know," Coach said. "And we're going to go out there and play this game—and *win* it. We won't know anything more until I hear from the committee."

"But when will that be?" Josh asked.

"Any minute now, I hope," Coach answered. "Listen, men. Let's keep our minds on the game. We can beat South Colby. In fact, we *have* to beat South Colby, if we want to make it to the championship. So let's get out on the ice and do it!"

Derrick hit the ice and skated out to the faceoff circle. He could tell that Coach Campbell was trying to sound as optimistic as possible. He knew that the Panthers should try to play as if there were no problem at all—but that wasn't easy. Especially because Derrick—and most of the Panther squad—were sure that their season was about to come to an early end.

"Things don't look very good, do they?" Woody asked, skating by with his stick in his hands.

"No," Derrick answered. "They sure don't."

Derrick lost the faceoff to the South Colby center. He watched Bannister lumber forward, poke-checking. The center just faked to the side and left

Bannister behind. Derrick raced into the Panther defensive zone to stop the drive, but the South Colby center lifted his stick and whacked a solid slap shot before Derrick or Sam could block him.

A.J. made a beautiful save in the goal, leaping to the side and snagging the puck in his glove, like a first baseman grabbing a sharp line drive. Derrick sped behind the goal, circled close to the net, and picked up the puck as A.J. dropped it to the ice.

All right, A.J.! Derrick thought as he stickhandled up ice.

Derrick passed the puck up to Woody, and Woody crossed the blue line. Immediately, Woody was checked by the left winger, and the puck drifted free. Derrick raced over and swept up the loose puck, and wound up to hit a slap shot. He felt his stick vibrate as it cracked against the ice. As soon as Derrick followed through, he knew that he had hit a lousy shot and missed a perfect scoring opportunity. The puck sailed far wide of the goal, smacked against the Plexiglas, and was picked up by a South Colby winger.

Derrick hoped the rest of the game wasn't going to be as bad as his shot. He straightened up on his skates, and turned back toward center ice as the winger stickhandled along the boards.

Derrick moved in against the winger, planning to slam him against the boards with a body check. Derrick crouched down, bent his knees, and aimed his shoulder at the South Colby player's chest. At the last minute, the player stopped on a dime, changed direction, and Derrick crashed into the boards. The winger cut around and passed the puck up ice, to the center who was waiting at the blue line.

Derrick could only watch as the center stickhandled right at A.J., faked a slap shot right, then crushed the puck into the high left corner of the goal—just beyond A.J.'s mitt.

When the second period ended, the Panthers walked into their locker room with the score South Colby 1, Alden 0. Coach hadn't heard anything from the committee yet, and the Panthers were playing like their season was over. Derrick leaned his stick against the lockers and slumped down on the long wooden bench, looking depressed.

"South Colby is putting up a good fight," Coach said to the team. "But we should be taking them to the cleaners. What's wrong out there?" Coach began pacing back and forth. "We're letting Colby dominate the game. We're not checking them enough in our own defensive zone, and we're letting them shoot easy shots. Bannister and Sam, you're both trying to check when you're the last person in front of our goal. Derrick, you're not hustling out there like you usually do."

Coach took a deep breath and stopped pacing. "I know it's not an easy time for the team," he continued. "But let's go out there and show South Colby our true colors. We have one period left. I know we can come back. So let's do it!"

As Derrick was skating around the ice, waiting for the faceoff to begin the third period, he looked into the section where Chris was sitting. Suddenly, his heart began to race. Coach Campbell was standing next to Chris, talking excitedly. Chris jumped up and down, gave Coach a little hug, and looked down at Derrick giving a big thumbs-up.

Derrick skated over to the Plexiglas.

"What's up?" he asked.

"Coach just got the call," Chris called back. "Next game, I'm allowed to play! The committee said we won't have to forfeit a single game!"

"Yes!" Derrick cried, lifting up his stick and smiling.

South Colby didn't know what hit them. Suddenly, the Panthers were a different team.

Josh checked the South Colby center, slamming

him into the boards, and picked up the loose puck right near the Panthers' goal. He passed up ice to Woody, who turned and skated along the left boards, crossing the blue line and trying to dodge clear of the South Colby defense. Derrick raced into the Panthers' offensive zone, ready to pick up a pass.

As soon as Derrick turned to cut in front of the goal, he knew that Woody would get the puck to him. Woody whacked the pass between the skates of the South Colby defenseman, and Derrick smiled to himself as he felt the puck slap against his stick. The Panthers were back!

Derrick faked a backhand wrist shot, forcing the goalie to lunge, then cut tightly around the back of the net. The goalie flopped back to the other side, to block Derrick's shot. Derrick came in tight along the side of the net, then pushed the puck back into the net for a classic wraparound goal.

"Yes!" Derrick cried, raising his arms and giving Woody a high five.

The score was tied, South Colby 1, Alden 1.

"Who wants to score the next goal?" Derrick said in a cocky voice, before the next faceoff.

"I think it's my turn," Josh answered with a smile.

"Josh gets to score the next goal," Derrick said, turning to the team.

Derrick won the faceoff, passing out to Woody. Woody took the puck across the blue line, and waited for Derrick and Josh to skate into position. Then Woody wound up and smacked a bee-line slap shot. The goalie dove to the side, knocking the puck with his stick hand. The shot rebounded right into Josh's stick. He flicked his wrist and the puck flew into the net, above the sprawled-out body of the South Colby goalie.

"Yeah Josh!" Derrick said, knocking his friend on the helmet. "Killer shot!"

The Panthers were having an amazing third period. Derrick wanted to make sure South Colby didn't get back in the game. He wanted to seal the game right then.

With thirty-seven seconds left in the third period, the puck was near the Panthers' goal. The South Colby center passed out to the left winger, who took a slap shot. A.J. deflected the puck with his stick, and Josh picked it up. He passed up ice to Derrick, who raced as fast as he could across the blue line, speeding past one defenseman, and dodging around the other with a perfect head fake.

It was just Derrick and the goalie, face to face. Derrick didn't want to get too close, so he faked a slap shot to the right, then flicked a wrist shot to the left. The goalie was fooled, and the puck shot into the net.

The Alden crowd went crazy, as Derrick skated back to center ice. Near the faceoff circle, he was met by Woody, Josh, and Sam. They formed a huddle and gave each other bear hugs and helmet-slaps.

"We did it!" Chris yelled from the stands.

"The Panthers rule!" Derrick shouted back.

13

Bannister cleared his throat, rapped his knuckles loudly on the table, then stood up. After the South Colby game most of the Panther squad gathered at Pete's Pizza for a victory feast. Derrick could tell that Bannister was about to give one of his famous speeches.

"I just have a few words to say," Bannister began, without smiling. "About Christina Mary Santini."

Chris blushed and kicked Bannister under the table, but Bannister kept right on talking. "We all know that Chris is a great member of our hockey team. We all know that she can play hockey as well as most boys. Except me, of course."

Everyone laughed, and threw wadded up napkins at Bannister's face.

"But there's one thing that I don't think Chris can do as well as boys," Bannister went on, trying not to smile. "And that is—eat."

Everyone laughed and clapped, and Bannister patted his big belly.

"Oh, yeah?" Chris said, snatching up a piece of pizza and shoving the whole thing in her mouth, till her cheeks were puffed up like a chipmunk.

"This is war!" Bannister said, grabbing his own piece of pizza and shoving it in his mouth.

Derrick laughed and watched Chris and Bannister eat two more pieces of pizza. He couldn't believe that a girl could eat as much as Bannister—"The Human Vacuum Cleaner." When Bannister reached for his fourth piece, Chris threw her napkin to the table in surrender.

"You win, Bannister," Chris said, slumping down into the chair. "I feel like I'm about to explode."

"Don't get sick, Chris," Derrick said. "We need you out on the ice. Not at home with a stomachache."

"Don't worry, I'll be there," Chris said. "I want to prove to the committee, and those Williamsport jerks, that girls can play hockey just as well as boys."

"We'll really need you out there if we're going to make it to the championship," Woody added.

Woody was making some calculations on the back of a napkin. He wrote a few more numbers, then put his pencil down.

"According to my calculations," Woody continued, "we have to win our last two games. Williamsport will make it to the championship if they win one of their next two games. And if North Colby beats South Colby, we may have to play a play-off game, or else add up total goals, subtract the number of minutes spent in the penalty box . . ."

"Okay, okay, we get the picture," Josh said, shaking his head. "The important thing is that we still have a chance to make it to the championship."

"I wouldn't mind playing Williamsport again," Derrick said. "I sure would like to have another shot at Schonberg."

Derrick knew that Schonberg was beating him in their race to win the conference high-scoring trophy. So far that season, Schonberg had scored fourteen goals, and Derrick had only scored eleven. Now that the Panthers were back together, Derrick couldn't wait for the chance to show Schonberg a thing or two about scoring goals.

"Let's just make sure we win these next two games," Chris said. She raised up her glass of soda and said, "To victory!"

"To victory!" all the Panthers answered.

And victory was exactly what the Panthers got. The Panthers blew Bradley off the ice, 4–0. Derrick scored two goals, Chris scored one, and Josh scored another one with a slap shot from the point.

Two days after the Bradley game, the Panthers walked all over Lincoln, 3–1. With that victory, the Panthers assured themselves of a spot in the championship against Williamsport.

Derrick was psyched. This was his chance to lead the Panthers to the conference title. When the championship game started, in the loud, crowded Williamsport Rink, Schonberg had sixteen goals on the season, and Derrick had fifteen.

Derrick knew exactly what he was up against. He just hoped he, and the Panthers, could do the job.

Derrick crashed against the boards. He felt Schonberg's shoulder driving into his back as he fought to keep possession of the puck.

"Looks like you guys got your girl back," Schonberg said. "We're still going to take you apart."

Schonberg pushed off Derrick and hooked the

puck, pulling it free. He passed it out to the Williamsport right winger, who turned and crossed the blue line.

The game was only two minutes old and things were already going badly for the Panthers. Williamsport had come out strong—skating fast, checking hard, and passing and shooting with deadly accuracy. The Williamsport right winger had already scored a goal, and it looked like he was on his way to a second.

Derrick rushed toward the puck, watching as Sam confronted the right winger. The winger stickhandled around Sam, and headed for the net. Derrick raced to get between the winger and the goal. He skidded to a stop right in front of A.J., just in time to stop the winger from shooting. Instead, the pass went across the ice to Schonberg, who delivered a blazing slap shot. A.J. deflected the puck with his chest, and Derrick tried to get to it. The winger beat him and flicked the puck over A.J.'s stick into the corner of the goal.

Suddenly, the score was Williamsport 2, Alden 0.

Schonberg had earned an assist on the play, and Derrick was relieved that Schonberg hadn't scored so far. The longer the Panthers shut out Schonberg, the better chance Derrick had of beating him. Still,

Derrick tried to keep his mind on winning the game first, not winning the title.

"What's wrong, Larson?" Schonberg said, as they faced each other in the faceoff circle. "Your girl player isn't helping you out very much, is she?"

Derrick felt his face get hot with anger. He kept his eyes right on Schonberg's, staring him down. As soon as the puck hit the ice, Derrick whacked Schonberg's stick out of the way and scooped the puck forward to Chris.

Schonberg followed Chris, poke checking and driving her toward the left boards. Derrick drove toward the goal, hoping that Chris would pass around Schonberg. But Schonberg laid his shoulder into Chris's side and drove her into the boards. He stole the puck from her and passed it up ice to the right winger. Sam caught the winger with a hip check, and the winger went up on one skate, before regaining his balance.

Derrick skated into the Panthers' defensive zone, breathing hard. Sam and Woody were double-teaming the winger, so Derrick covered the zone that stretched up the middle of the ice. The winger passed the puck behind the net, across the middle to the left winger in the far corner. Derrick shifted toward the puck, then burst forward when the winger passed up ice to the Williamsport defenseman at the point.

Derrick saw the defenseman take his stick back for a slap shot. The puck went zooming by his shoulder, and Derrick decided to keep right on skating— hoping that a rebound, and a quick pass, could develop into a Panther breakaway.

He skated toward the center line, looking behind him like a wide receiver looking for a football. A.J. blocked the shot, and Chris picked up the puck. She quickly smacked it up ice right into Derrick's stick. Two steps later, Derrick was across the blue line all alone. It was a classic breakaway—Derrick against the Williamsport goalie.

Things don't get any easier than this, Derrick thought as he sped forward, stickhandling. *If you miss this, you're in real trouble.*

Derrick faked left, then smacked the puck to the right. The puck went sailing wide of the goal. Derrick shook his head in disgust and picked up the puck, but the Williamsport defense was already on him, and the best scoring opportunity of the game had been wasted.

A few seconds later, the first period ended with the score still Williamsport 2, Alden 0.

14

"What's the problem out there, Panthers?" Coach Campbell asked, in the locker room. Chris always hung out in the boys' locker room between periods. She was sitting next to Derrick and Josh, taping the blade of her stick.

"If you ask me," Coach went on, "we're playing like a bunch of girls out there."

Chris's head popped up, and she looked at Coach with an angry expression.

"Sorry, Chris," Coach said, shaking his head. "For a second there, I forgot you were a girl."

Derrick and Josh had to bite their tongues to keep from laughing. Coach gave them a serious glance. Laughing was okay when you were way ahead, but when you were behind—especially in the championship game—it was time to get serious.

"I hope you're laughing when the game is over," Coach said, starting to pace up and down the aisle. "We've got to get into gear, Panthers. There's plenty of time in the game. But we're not taking advantage of big plays. We're not taking shots when we're open for shots. Remember, if you're open for a shot—take it. Don't pass unless you think someone else is going to have a better shot on goal than you. We won't score unless we shoot."

Derrick led the team back onto the ice.

"I can't believe Coach actually said that we're playing like a bunch of girls," Chris said, as they skated around the rink, waiting for the faceoff.

"Well, don't get mad at Coach," Derrick said. "Get mad at Schonberg. He's the one who thinks we can't beat Williamsport because we have a girl on our team."

"What a jerk!" Chris answered.

Derrick could tell that Chris was riled up. She

skated around the ice, whacking her stick against the boards. Derrick smiled to himself. Maybe Chris could get the Panthers psyched to come back.

A minute later, Schonberg was working the puck out of the corner. A.J. was tight against the side of the goal, one arm clasping the goalpost, both legs bent and ready to spring. Josh was covering Schonberg, driving him deeper into the corner.

Schonberg stopped fast, cut, and charged toward the goal, trying for a wraparound shot. Josh ducked his shoulder and dug it into Schonberg's chest before he could get past. Derrick could see the look of surprise on Schonberg's face when he felt the power of Josh's body check. Schonberg went up on one skate, then fell over backward, landing on his back.

Chris picked up the loose puck and stickhandled through the Williamsport defense, while Derrick sped ahead of her toward the blue line. Chris whacked a perfect pass to Derrick, and Derrick sped into the Williamsport defensive zone, stickhandling closer to the goal. The defenseman was skating backward, poke-checking with his stick. Derrick faked around him, lifted his stick, and creamed the puck at the high left corner of the goal.

Derrick knew that he had hit a great shot. The Williamsport goalie flopped to the side, thrusting his thick goalie's stick into the air—but the puck slipped in for a goal.

"Great pass!" Derrick yelled to Chris.

The score was now Williamsport 2, Alden 1. And with Derrick's goal, both he and Schonberg had sixteen goals for the season. The last thing Derrick wanted was to tie with Schonberg for the trophy. As far as Derrick was concerned, it was all or nothing.

And Derrick wanted it all.

With one minute left in the second period, Schonberg was skating along the boards with the puck. Derrick was on him in a flash, poke-checking. When Schonberg stopped quick and tried to cut toward center ice, Derrick rammed his shoulder into Schonberg's side. Schonberg didn't budge, and the two boys leaned against each other, fighting for the puck.

"You might as well just give up," Schonberg muttered, as they whacked at the puck and rammed each other with their shoulders.

Derrick didn't answer. While Schonberg was talking, Derrick swept the puck free with his blade, and passed it clear. Woody picked up the pass and took it across the blue line, with Derrick and Chris charging right behind him.

Woody met the defenseman head-on, and right be-

fore they crashed into each other, he dropped a pass
back to Derrick. Derrick didn't stop the puck. He just
took his stick back and whacked the pass toward the
goal.

The Williamsport goalie knocked the puck away
with his pads. Chris was still speeding in toward the
goal, along the left boards. The goalie scrambled out
to dive on the puck, but Chris scooped it up first. She
pulled it away from the goalie's mitt, then skated
right past the side of the goal—dropping the puck
into the net as she passed.

The Alden fans exploded, and Chris was mobbed
by the team. When the buzzer sounded to end the
second period, the score was all tied up, 2–2.

Derrick skated up to the faceoff circle and took a
deep breath. There were only twenty seconds left in
the game, and the score was still tied at 2–2. Derrick
knew that everything came down to these last few
moments of play. If Derrick could get the puck into
the net, the Panthers would win the championship,
and he'd win the high-scoring trophy.

If Schonberg scored, Derrick and the Panthers
would be left empty-handed.

Schonberg skated up, bent his knees, and put his

blade on the ice. They were facing-off in the Panthers' defensive zone, and A.J. was guarding the goal with his life. Derrick felt his heart pounding like crazy, as the referee dropped the puck into the circle.

Schonberg won the faceoff, knocking the puck back to his right winger. The winger whacked a quick slap shot, but A.J. blocked it. Schonberg was there to get the rebound. He flicked it up, past A.J.'s glove, and Derrick felt his stomach sink.

But the puck smacked the top post of the goal, and deflected straight up into the air. Derrick smiled as he watched A.J. catch the puck as if it were a pop fly. It was a lucky break. He turned and skated up ice, as A.J. dropped the puck for Chris.

Derrick stopped at the blue line and watched Chris stickhandle into the Williamsport defensive zone. He followed after her, as she cut and dodged toward the goal. Schonberg was skating right next to Derrick, trying to catch up with Chris—but there was nothing he could do. Chris was too fast.

There were less than ten seconds left and the crowd was on its feet, cheering louder than anything Derrick had ever heard.

Both Williamsport defensemen converged on Chris, taking her out of the play with a set of nasty body checks. Before she went down, Chris dropped a pass back to Derrick. Derrick and Schonberg were both going for the puck, but Derrick knocked Schonberg to the ice with a perfectly timed body check. The puck was his.

He stickhandled past the two defensemen, and lifted the puck into the corner of the net—just as the buzzer sounded.

The Alden fans went wild. The whole team was out on the ice a moment later, mobbing Derrick and Chris.

"Ladies and gentlemen," the announcer said over the loudspeakers, "the Alden Panthers are the new conference champions! And Derrick Larson has just won the conference high-scoring trophy. Congratulations to the Panthers, and to Derrick!"

The huddle parted, and Derrick skated toward the announcer's table. There was a huge trophy sitting on the table, shining in the light. As he reached for the trophy, Derrick caught a glimpse of Schonberg, skating back toward the Williamsport locker room. He was tempted to turn around and make some last-minute comment to Schonberg—but he decided it wasn't worth the trouble.

"You deserve part of this trophy, too," Derrick said

to Chris, as she skated up to give him a high five. "You were the one who gave me all those great assists."

"But you're the one who scored," Chris said with a huge smile.

Derrick smiled, too, took the trophy, and lifted it high above his head.

Pro Set Cards
and the
Alden All Stars
present
THE ALL STAR SWEEPSTAKES

- **Grand Prize: a trip for two to the 1992 Pro Bowl in Hawaii**

- **First Prize: a *complete* set of Pro Set's 1991 Series I and II—the *official* card of the NFL. Complete sets are not available in stores.**

- **Two Second Prizes: all of the books in the Alden All Stars series—nine books in all!**

OFFICIAL RULES—NO PURCHASE NECESSARY

1. On an official entry form, print your name, address, zip code, and age. Use the entry form printed below, or you may obtain an entry form and a set of rules by sending a self-addressed stamped envelope to: ALL STAR SWEEPSTAKES, P.O. Box 655, Sayreville, NJ 08871. Residents of WA and VT need not include postage. Requests must be received by October 15, 1991.
2. Enter as often as you wish, but each entry must be mailed separately to ALL STAR SWEEPSTAKES, P.O. Box 516, Sayreville, NJ 08871. No mechanically reproduced entries will be accepted. All entries must be received by November 30, 1991.
3. Winners will be selected from among all eligible entries received, in a random drawing conducted by Marden-Kane Inc., an independent judging organization whose decisions are final in all matters relating to this sweepstakes. All prizes will be awarded and winners notified by mail. Prizes are nontransferable, and no substitutions or cash equivalents are allowed. Taxes, if any, are the responsibility of the winners. Winners may be asked to execute an affidavit of eligibility and release. No responsibility is assumed for lost or misdirected mail. Grand Prize consists of a four-night/five-day trip for two to the 1992 Pro Bowl in Hawaii, including round-trip air transportation, hotel accommodations, game tickets, hotel-to-game and hotel-to-airport transfers, breakfasts and dinners. In the event that the trip is won by a minor, it will be awarded in the name of a parent or legal guardian. Trip must be taken on date specified or the prize will be forfeited and an alternate winner selected. Approximate retail value of the Grand Prize is $3500. First Prize consists of a complete set of Pro Set's 1991 series I and II football cards. Pro Set cards are the official card of the NFL and complete sets are not available in stores. Two second prizes consist of a complete set of the Alden All Stars series, constituting nine books as of the time of the drawing. Approximate retail value of each of the Second Prizes is $50. PENGUIN USA and its affiliates reserve the right to use the prize winners' names and likenesses in any promotional activities relating to this sweepstakes without further compensation to the winners.
4. This Sweepstakes is open to residents of the U.S. only. Employees and their families of PENGUIN USA and its affiliates, advertising/promotion agencies, and retailers, and employees of Daniel Weiss Associates, Inc. may not enter. This offer is void wherever prohibited and subject to all federal, state, and local laws. NFL Properties is not a sponsor nor endorses this sweepstakes.
5. For a list of winners, send a stamped, self-addressed envelope to ALL STAR SWEEPSTAKES WINNERS, P.O. Box 705, Sayreville, NJ 08871.

ALL STAR SWEEPSTAKES OFFICIAL ENTRY FORM

Name _____ Age _____

Address _____

City/State/ZIP _____

(please print)